MEANINGFUL WORK

MEANINGFUL WORK

JoAnna Novak

STORIES

TUSCALOOSA

FC2 is an imprint of the University of Alabama Press

Inquiries about reproducing material from this work should be addressed
to the University of Alabama Press

Book Design: Publications Unit, Department of English, Illinois State
    University; Director: Steve Halle Production Assistant: Pearl Osibu
Cover image: Mitchell Luo, unsplash.com
Cover Design: Lou Robinson
Typeface: Adobe Caslon Pro

Library of Congress Cataloging-in-Publication Data is available from
the Library of Congress.

ISBN: 978-1-57366-191-1
E-ISBN: 978-1-57366-893-4

Works Cited
Ronald Fraser, *Blood of Spain: An Oral History of the Spanish Civil War*
    (New York: Pantheon, 1979), 309.
Kerri Webster, "Vanitas", from *The Trailhead* (Wesleyan, 2018), 63.

To Thomas

Contents

The ground was hard, the air was still, my road was lonely; I walked fast till I got warm, and then I walked slowly to enjoy and analyze the species of pleasure brooding for me in the hour and situation.

—Charlotte Brontë, *Jane Eyre*

However once you get used to living life with your heart in your throat you get used to it.

—H. G. Carrillo, *Loosing My Espanish*

The Wait

The moist cheese on his blue-and-white porcelain, the Pinot.

Our entire marriage, I had been accepting those gifts, not waiting for the meal. My husband came into the living room and sniffed behind my ear. He moved my pretty hair. He told me I smelled like a newborn. Not baby powder: it was something else about me.

Did you ever find pineapples? he asked. For Sunday?

No.

You better go back. Otherwise it's on the list with the playing cards.

What?

I'm kidding, he said.

He handed me that sweaty cheese.

I want to wait for dinner, I said. He left the wine on the arm of the sofa. I sat there, watching the kitchen fill with steam.

And that's how I coddled the wait. It was a misfit infant coming, no matter how slowly or quickly I ate my supper.

Both this phantom infant and I wanted to separate from my husband.

You'll get your wish, I told the infant.

I poured the wine my husband gave me out the window, where it ran red on the asphalt.

A turgid thunk came from the kitchen: that was my husband, slow at the cutting board.

Meanwhile, the wait was developing a smell, of starch coming off pasta. And it had its sound, the hidden purr of boiling water. Our timer was a cat, one of those Japanese good luck charms with crazy eyes.

It rang and the pasta was poured into a colander.

I did not need to be in the kitchen with my husband to know that he was waiting for the water to run off the noodles before he returned them to the pot. Shook them. Sauced them.

We were not waiting for the same thing, and perhaps we never had been. Except, perhaps, once. There was the time he had told me to undress and crawl from the kitchen to the bedroom so he could watch my ass, to wait for him at the foot of the bed, on all fours. I did.

Then it was dinner. Absolutely, the wait was there, sitting at the table like an awful baby or a pepper mill. I could not tell if it was across from me, around me, riding my back like a coat.

Heat rose off the noodles, and I fought back speech.

The food was still too warm to taste. I needed something for my mouth. The wine, I guess. The sheep's Brie I'd turned down. Perhaps I'd developed this tendency in the early days of love when we'd waited out halftime ads, his penis in my mouth.

By "tendency," I probably mean "habit."

Ritual, like whacking your thumb every morning with a hammer and hiding the pain with your tongue.

Ten faces, ten colors, my husband said, looking at me looking at my food. It was a common saying in Japan, and he'd been using it since he was twenty, when he'd spent a year there doing voice work for a pocket-dictionary publisher. He held up his glass and went on: to us and our missing pineapple and our cat egg timer.

Damn he was good. He toasted every night, and here I was, waiting for a noodle to leap off the table. I dawdled with my fork.

Is it alright? he asked.

Just not hungry, I said.

I dabbed my mouth with my napkin and got it red.

All along, I hadn't been waiting but awaiting. I was awaiting discovery, awaiting someone who would sweep up all my crumbs and recreate a cake. I had ruined the napkin. I had tossed the wine.

What would I have to do?

I'm waiting, my husband said, drawing out the word, singsong.

Waiting, awaiting.

Now, when you bring me to your different bed, I slow myself from desiring you, new person. Ceremony, like patience, is a dark art. Two bodies needn't share a meal. I ask you to crawl for me, come for me, and I am so hopeful with my flat, empty stomach. When it starts to talk, I tell myself to keep waiting. That's it. I wait for everything you do.

Meaningful Work

Pre-shift you stop at Valley Mart. You need two Mountain Dews to survive. The slog. You'll slug Dew—wind catching your black chef pants, raw chicken gunking your kitchen clogs—and mud will pour into the Mansion. Gray-brown, doom and gloom, life after your mother's death—this is what you need to overcome: today's shift. Tell yourself it's any Tuesday.

You wear your mom's ashes in a fish-eye marble around your neck. What that, Miguel asked your first day at the Mansion. You glared at him and his clouded iris. Only Zach had attended your mom's service. He's a good guy, according to your dad. I don't worry about sending you to work for Zach Brown.

Valley Mart is next to the monument shop. You park in front of their tacky display headstones, staked benignly in a rug of green-green lawn, the brightest on the block. None of the stones look right for your dad. So awful they beg you to stare. Like any ugly thing. They come in black, gray, red of sun-faded blood, molar white. Worst, with images: tranquil deer, thorny rose, treble cleft, hunched angel. Generic surnames etched in available fonts.

SMITH   *Jones*   Brown

Brown, brown, Zach Brown. At first you were just his former-boss's daughter; now you're JoAnimal, and he's got you wrapped around his finger, running around his kitchen like the floor is on fire.

We're all going sometime, your dad likes to say, cleaning the fish tank or charring toast, walking you to the door. His skin is smoke-sallow since he started buying cartons. Winstons. He keeps trying to find an afternoon when you can accompany him tombstone shopping, and you keep avoiding it, picking up extra Mansion shifts that jam your pulse in your throat. The memorial you choose is a personal declaration, reads the booklet your dad showed you. The limit is set only by your imagination.

Polishing display headstones must be someone's job, you realize in front of the lawn, the monuments buffed. You're reflected from the waist down in their faces—slim body, bones and joints and muscles and fat and flesh and skin. When your dad goes, his concrete upkeep is on you. It will be you who ensures his headstone is weed free, bird shit free, neat. Toothpicks his letters' crevices. Working at the Mansion has taught you: Certain pots never come clean. Anglaise comes in a squeeze jar. And mourning agrees with you, i.e., emotion agrees with you—the more you feel, the less you need. Also, you can eat off anything.

#

The monument shop and Valley Mart are on the corner of Mill Street. Traffic heads to the interstate, down the road that spans Franklin and Hampshire counties, probably further. You don't go further. Enter Valley Mart so you can buy your Dews and drive to work.

The clerk doesn't look up. She has pink hair. She picks at her phone with jaguar-print nails. At the Mansion, the servers wear blingy manicures, white-tipped, neon, rhinestoned; you envy them. You are a girl, too, one of the only girls working in the kitchen. You miss having nails. Well, you miss clean nails. Mushroom dirt, potato dirt won't wash off with a brush.

Your palms are sewn with crud.

DEW is 2 FOR $1.99, any color. Voltage, Revolution, Code Red. Plain sewage green. White Out reminds you of sixth grade, which seems a lot longer than ten years ago. When's time going to speed up? Tracey Picek painted her nails with Wite-Out and, with her buckteeth, ate it off.

Twenty-two months that you've worked at the Mansion: it feels that long.

"Anything else, hon?"

WORMS + CRAWLRS advertised in bubble-lettered signs Scotch-taped to the counter. The tape is peeling. The writing is highlighter orange.

You could bring Chef a Red Bull. You could text him. You could say meet me at my car. Meet me behind the funeral parlor. Meet me in your street clothes. Let's take off. Let's get lost. You should text him: Will you or won't you? You don't. You shake your head.

"Two and two," says the girl, flashing nubby teeth.

#

June, and the low's eighty, murk overtaken by a fat sun. You too could be eclipsable. Present-you. Now-you. In the kitchen, you eclipsed your father. At a red light, you stare at the labels. Arctic Burst, not White Out. For a minute that makes more sense. Your AC is shot: the vents leak a smell like athlete's foot.

The Dews sweat in the cupholders, soaking gum wrappers and receipts. Why is condensation so gross? Like handicapped bathrooms and chicken skin. It's water, it's natural, you think, but nausea crawls in your mouth when you touch the wet paper.

After Labor Day, you'll start at GCC. Two seminars, two labs. If classes go okay, after the first term you'll get an externship at the country club or the bistro in Shelburne Falls where you ate before prom, somewhere good, better than the Mansion. Two years, you'll be certified. You could move out of your dad's apartment/sadness/shadow and work in a real kitchen in a real city by water more than the Connecticut River. You could stop pining over the chef. In the meantime, you're six days a week on hors d'oeuvres at the Mansion, and it's wedding season.

The only wedding you've ever attended was your mom's creepy brother's. It was a second wedding, which is right there with bottle-sweat-handicap-chicken, or at least this one was. It was awkwardly small, in Turners, at your uncle's prefab yellow house, a mountain of trash glaring down on the backyard and a white tent staked into the patchy grass and five or six of those round eight-tops covered in checkered plastic, red and white. Hamburgers and hotdogs and foil things of pork 'n' beans, coleslaw, browning lettuce, crinkle-cut cukes.

Tony used to be a heartbreaker, your mom said in the car. She brayed. When she was doing all right, her voice was louder. Tony was her only brother, so she abhorred and adored him. Now he's a pharmacist.

Crossing the bridge over the falls, the water splashed like frothy ice; it hit the river so blue, it looked fake. You were thirteen. Your mom was maybe fine. She dragged her garden salad through a blob of French and split your chocolate-chocolate cupcake, the frosting.

Why he's marrying a troll, I can't tell you, she said, almost shouting. The bride looked like a mole rat in Lennon glasses.

Nance, your dad said, winking. Be a little kind.

He watched her for you.

The Mansion is the opposite direction of Turners. A few years after the wedding, Tony and the mole rat moved to Iowa—to drown in cows and corn and cheese curds, your mom said. When Mom died, Tony and the mole rat didn't send flowers, not even a card. Well, they missed your graduation too. Your mom's family always doubted her, your dad said, in whiskey moments, those first days after, when it was suddenly June and for the first time ever you two were alone. They expected your mom to go, Tony did, he wanted her to give up. And Laurie—she's a piece of work. A nurse? Nurse Ratched. Give me a break.

(For your last birthday, she'd sent you a book about how family members could cope with their loved one's eating disorders.)

When you came home from Williams, at the end of your second year, you dated a guy in Turners. He was nothing. Horror movies and vodka-sodas and a lot of couch fucking. When you'd go to his place you looked for that house where the wedding was, the Styrofoam plates, the trash heap, just to find something from when your mom was still alive. Just anything familiar. You never found it. You were done with liberal arts. Also the past. It was condemned or razed, something from your imagination.

#

The union of creepy Uncle Tony and the mole rat had been one of shittiness and middle-aged convenience. Mansion couples are in love. They're young enough to want three hundred invites to ogle their nuptial bliss. Choices aren't yet hassles, but chances. They're drunk off a future overflowing with what's possible, like your mom and dad in photos on the mantel: smiley, playful, touchy, easy-skinny. The sunset surges pink and orange and purple hopes. Waists are nipped. A convertible dangles streamers and beer cans.

Sometimes you see the newlyweds. You feel like an anthropologist in the bush. When you help the servers set up or if the reception comes with a station: Retro Diner Midnight (hotdogs, mini-burgers, onion rings) or Fancy Sundae Bar or Fresh-Carved Sirloin. Brides alternate between simpering and snippy; grooms are booze-flushed and benign. You never imagined a ceremony; you never tried on someone else's last name; and these days, when you see the room all decked out before the reception, the centerpieces dripping baby's breath and greenery, the tables strewn with pearlescent confetti or ivory beads, you feel crone-ish. Depraved. You want everything bruised and rushed and rash.

To the future! Dudes are always toasting as you're making your way to the veranda or the hot food buffet. The guests tear, gleamy. The future is the time when you will be more what you've already become.

#

Employees park behind the funeral home across the street from the Mansion. Everyone except Zach; his truck goes on the other side of the building, in a gravel drive next to the loading dock by the river.

Even funerals require dumpsters—for old bouquets and punctured coffee pods and stale cookie platters and the cardboard tabs inside men's collars and many, many tissues.

Not bodies.

The average adult human takes two to two-and-a-half hours to complete their burn, you read in one of five large-print pamphlets while you stared at your legs and listened to your dad stammer.

She didn't want to be . . . in the ground, he said to the goateed cremation consultant, whose expression confirmed he'd heard it all before. A body in a plot does that. She doesn't want us tied to any one place.

Was it wrong to be wearing jean shorts at this appointment? You could just hear your mother: Look how fat thighs get when you're sitting down. Who wants to be an average adult?

(With your mom, all adjectives secretly described size. *Healthy* was her least favorite word.)

After the cremator, your mom was ash and bone; after the processor, she was nothing more than a couple uniform quarts.

Like putting gravel in a blender, the cremation consultant said. That's crude, but don't diamonds come from rocks?

The front of the Mansion is weepy blue; the back, salmon. Be careful with yourself, your dad says. Young guns go whipping through. You, too, whip through, watching for other yous—front-of-the-house you, garde-manger-you, bakeshop-you, grill-you, custodial-you—as you turn into the lot.

In your car, you sit with the windows up, heat mounting, eighties music—Eddie Money blasting—I have a hunger, it's a hunger. Your life has been stalled ever since. You slip your mom under your tank top. Today is two years. Her body burned in an hour. A weight between your breasts, a lump clogging your throat. You text your dad: arrived. You lick the corners of your mouth for dried toothpaste. His reply comes quick: Thanks, sweetie. Hang in there today. You're fine. You're good.

#

The Mansion lot is packed. That means a luncheon, plus guests at the attached inn, which is chintzy, sprawling, unaffiliated with a chain, susceptible to erratic decor. Year-round Christmas lights. Fake ivy vines. A waterfront patio shaded by river birches. The banquet halls are mauve and turquoise with Greco-Roman trompe l'oeil columns; the women's lounge is a Victorian pleasure bower. You've never seen a guest room.

Amidst the cars, beneath a cloud-blank sky, you feel the pull, a yanking wince behind your eyes, satellites of your heart: to turn and speed-walk away, fast, calves burning, faster, your mother told you, don't dillydally, and seal yourself in your car, silence, heat, nothing, no one, then succumb to noise and cross the Connecticut River and consider swerving into the concrete guardrail (you consider this every day) and crack the first Dew and veer toward the interstate and go to the mall and wander like time's not precious, buy actual pants, or better, a skirt, and throw out your chefwear, leave your panties in the dressing room, smash your phone and forget your texts, fill up the tank with premium gas and buy cigarettes and Flamin' Hot Cheetos and a handful of scratch-offs, forget your dad and his morbid desire to pre-plan, and forget your mom, that her mordant overgrown-adolescent-self ever existed, and forget you tried college, forget your whiling-away chef crush, drive for days and nights and the no-person's time of sleeplessness and hunger and thirst, piss in a bottle, sleep in your car, do roadside push-ups to wake yourself up, bang a lot lizard (you can be into girls), try on a sexy-nice androgynous name (James) when you check in under an alias at a throwback motel with spotty premium cable and maybe a kidney-shaped pool, Do Not Disturb signs doodled with bonneted maids, and use up your breaths disintegrating into a jobless, toothless hag too weak and daffy to fuck or text or sharpen a knife.

But you don't get paid until Friday. And maybe your dad needs you. Escape is what you want when you don't really know what you want.

Past the dumpsters and walk-in #6 and freezer #2 and the semicircle of royal-blue milk crates and the cluster of rolling racks and the narrow passage—one way leads behind the building to the riverbank, the other behind #6, past metal tubes and boxes, past the walk-in, to a clearing where guys sit and smoke—the kitchen door is open.

#

"There she is, there she is," says ebullient Kurt. His face is pieces through the space between the stainless-steel shelves. He has a wide nose and tattoos of his three daughters' names up his right forearm—the middle girl is his favorite. She gets the best phone.

"Hola, JoAní!" Miguel says, pushing a metal oar around the kettle. He leans over and you fist-pound; it took eleven months for you to be friends. Now you know things. Miguel is from Puerto Rico. The cloud fogging his right pupil is a disease he inherited from his father, his father's father, etc. He's been clean ten years, sous for nine, and he likes to rhumba with his wife. The kettle's not really a kettle: it's a metal bathtub-shaped vessel where he makes fifty-gallon batches of bland marinara.

On grill #1 is Dwayne, a registered sex offender in his fifties who abuses his cat. Grill #2 is MK, dying of brain cancer but begging to work. Beneath his skullcap his actual skull is knit with surgery scars. He is your-mom-at-the-end gaunt: gross-thin, too thin for a casket. Grill #3 is Oliver; he's like a work older brother, but flirty. You can flirt with anyone you're not into. Oliver has a buzz that makes his head look like a penis. He shoots rifles and goes skiing, takes blonds on sushi dates, and lives with his grandma.

Chef station, in front of grill #1, used to be your dad's, before your mom's last month. Your dad is how you got into the Mansion at the end of that summer, when you realized you weren't leaving home. Together, you'd moved into a two-bedroom. Kitchen, bathroom, bedroom, bedroom, family room: plenty. You couldn't handle a campus. School could wait. Wait wait wait until the registrar lost your records and the number on your ID evaporated.

Chef station pre-your-dad was Crazy Freddie: a one-armed, one-eyed dynamo, a living, blinking (just the one eye) POW. Now chef station belongs to Zach: his cutting board, his stack of perfectly flat folded rag towels, his silver thermos of black coffee, his tidy celery dice.

"What's good?" says Steph, the other girl in banquets. The bakery downstairs is packed with large-hipped matrons, but you've only got Steph to commiserate with about PMS in the kitchen heat (it's worse). She's whisking olive oil into a bowl of mayonnaise at the hors d'oeuvres station you share. The mixture gets yellower. She sets down the whisk and holds up a fleshy brown hand.

"Girl," you say, setting your Mountain Dews next to the cocktail picks and Steph's phone playing Daft Punk on the shelf.

You're short; Steph is maybe a midget, even in chef clogs. Can you ask that? She's your friend: she told you what tore when she gave birth. Steph is tubby with buzzed hair; your age, but she has two-year-old Calliope and a boyfriend and an exciting home life: days off, she cooks things like duck-egg pound cake and bulgogi.

On the hotbox next to your station, your list from yesterday has counts for the week. You scan the kitchen. Dishes accumulate at both dish pits, and in his black-and-whites Jason, the skeezy beverage manager, scoops ice.

"Where's Zach?"

"Downstairs?" Steph says. "I honestly don't know. Haven't seen the guy."

Here, Zach said yesterday, handing you a legal pad and a dull pencil. These are the parties. Figure out what you're gonna need. He pulled out the swivel chair at his half-desk, a glassed-in box across from his station and grill #1, and closed the door.

Inside his office, the kitchen sounds were muffled. You rolled up the sleeves of your chef coat and slipped your stockinged feet out of your clogs and pointed and flexed your toes and felt the always-astonishing pleasure of sitting mid-shift. Above you, stuff too expensive for dry storage: saffron threads, vanilla beans, jarred truffles. You heard your breath. As you tallied up the number of guests and the number of parties, the weddings per day that had ordered Brie-pear purses, sesame chicken, asparagus in phyllo, stuffed mushrooms, mini margaritas, lamb chops with maple mustard, short ribs and sushi and samosas, you lifted your gaze from time to time to look through the glass and watch for him watching you.

#

"Hey there, gorgeous," says Snoop in the basement. Rasta from his phone bumps out a scratched-up boom box on the counter, next to a cutout of when-she-was-still-skinny Tyra Banks, oiled up in a snakeskin bikini. Even her eyes look like they could yank you from the garden: dilated and green-apple green. A rack of cold salads and rainbow crudités.

Everyone has a nickname, but Snoop is Snoop because he's a sex offender and he's young: anonymity means he still has a chance with the servers. When you punch in, you're one of two hundred employees and you couldn't look up his name to research his crime if you wanted to. You have no clue about his last name. "You helpin' me?"

"I don't know," you say. "Where's Zach?"

Dwayne's record you checked. Watch out for him, your dad said, he's a prick. After your mom died, niceties disappeared. Your dad leveled. You've gotta be friendlier, he said when you came home from your first shift crying. Your mom was big on that standoffish thing. You're not in a classroom anymore. This isn't symposium. Guys'll think you're a bitch, sweetie. And just like I'm telling you Dwayne's a total dick, you don't want to be a total bitch. You treat people how you wanna be treated.

What you couldn't tell your dad was that you didn't know if you wanted guys to be dicks to you. Sometimes it felt good to cry or be treated like shit. Sometimes it felt good to make someone else feel bad, like Benny, who claimed to be an opera singer back in the DR but now was annoying and fat and, according to Miguel—Benny, he love you. Knowing that he liked you, you made Benny pre-fry all your vegetable spring rolls just so you wouldn't stink like Fry-o-lator. And then when he got them too dark, you acted like a bitch, which, the bad feeling, the guilt, you waited for it to sink in, but you just kept waiting.

Snoop spatulas hummus into two eye-shaped bowls. He scrapes the blades of the buffalo chopper clean.

"Zachy, Zachy, Zach," he says, gaze on the counter. He pauses, purses his lips. "I don't even know."

At night, when you got home, you read about Dwayne's convictions on your phone. A street-view map of the county popped up. A sex offender lived just down the block, between you and your dad's apartment and the retirement home.

"Let me find out," you say to Snoop, laughing for no reason. Friendliness means giggling and smiling and joking and high-fiving without a second thought. "Let me get back to you."

In the locker room, you search for a dishwasher's shirt amongst the chef coats. L, XL, XXL: all men's. You swim in an L. Most days, you borrow one from Zach: he's a medium, barely five-ten in Nikes. He doesn't wear chef clogs. Underneath his coat: a tight white T-shirt.

(His chef coats are embroidered with his name, the stitching sits on your left breast, or your left breast through bra and black tank top, Zach Brown. *Read me!*, you want to say.)

Long sleeves: brutal, cumbersome, always dragging through plates. Polyester doesn't breathe. The dishwasher shirts are short-sleeved, better. They snap up, which passes for sexy. Your arms. There aren't other skinny girls in the kitchen. You jam your bag in your locker; you check your phone. The nothing disappoints you. Sometimes you still expect an inept message from your mom: Don't eat 2 much pork or Gr8 job on ur lit ppr! Sometimes you're running late, just so you can text Zach and get back an Okay and totally lose your appetite. Dwayne molested a twelve-year-old boy and was in prison for fifteen years.

You, too, are taller in chef shoes.

#

Now you and Snoop are cool. It just took time. A few months. One shift, when you were facing a wall, washing heads of Bibb lettuce for a private party (Russians who only drank Cristal and Stolichnaya), mind off, not in the kitchen, Rihanna radio—we found love in a hopeless place—mind on sucking in your stomach, washing lettuce so quickly and thoroughly that Zach would see how fast/focused/knock-out you could be in your better-than-anyone concentration, so he could see, wow, she's really intense but in a good way, which even your dad told you was important, don't act like an airhead, Jo, those servers are more than enough trouble for anyone, it's not fair, no, look, it's not fair, but as a woman—yes, as a woman—you're going to have to work twice as hard in the kitchen, even if the guys try to tell you otherwise. I don't care how heavy that pot is, you lift it. Those sheet trays, those boxes—okay, and don't get offended if someone asks if you need help. You smile, say thank you, all right, maybe let them lighten your load, but you sure as hell don't go whining about it, not that you would, sweetie, but you just—there's biases, conscious or—and the cold water poured over your fingers, your fingers shrinking in the cold, and the grill searing and oven doors swinging and squeaking and that's when you felt it. Two hands on your head, settling in for a scalp massage.

Hey, pretty mama, you heard Snoop say, and you screamed. You couldn't stop yourself. You were frightened. Your heart pounded. As though you were suddenly alone, not in the kitchen, not surrounded by men; as though you were any girl, anywhere, behind a closed door.

What the fuck is wrong with you? you said, panting. Cold water pummeled the lettuce waiting in the sink. It was so delicate, the leaves would be bruised with forest-green teardrops.

Honey, hey, hey, Zach said, wiping his hands in a towel. He walked like a wind-up toy, unless he ran. What's going on, what's going on?

Snoop had his hands in the air and a not-this, not-me expression on his face.

I scared her, he said, backing up. I was just messing around. Gonna ask if she needed help. My bad, my bad.

Zach nodded. He looked at you, assessing. In the thick of that moment, when you felt like there wasn't one more emotion you could possibly be experiencing, something in Zach's seriousness made you think he got you: did he know that? You pretended his face wasn't his face; he wasn't hot when you really saw him. He just stood there, bug-eyed and quiet.

I'm sorry, baby. I swear. We good? Snoop said.

You sniffled. You turned off the water.

#

Upstairs, no Zach. You look for Miguel, who's moved twelve feet, from the kettle to the stock vat. The stock vat is taller than you, and it ends in a spigot that spits out smelly broth like bad breath.

"Hola, guapita," he says. "How you doing? You okay?"

"Better than okay," you say because now you know. If you're sad, pretend you're not. Scared, no way. If you're hungry, pretend you're full. If your mom died two years ago today, pretend that every shift isn't a dice roll of grief's five stages. Lose your mood at the door. "Where's Zach?"

"Zachy, he meet with Val," says Miguel. "Upstairs."

You nod.

"Chisme?"

Without teeth, Miguel's smile erases his lips. He opens his mouth.

"They fucking," he says, quiet and serious, watching your eyes. You remember how a week ago, when you brought Miguel a Red Bull so you weren't just bringing one for Zach, he pulled you aside when the kitchen was quiet and said: There anyone you like? Anyone you watch, JoAní?

Uh-uh, no way, no. But it feels so big inside you, of course he must know. Everyone probably does. Maybe you should talk to your dad.

"Ella es gorda como un cerdo. Oink, oink."

He cackles. He holds out his fist.

Pound.

"Boom!" he says. "Boom city!"

Everyone checks with Chef before beginning work. That's basic kitchen respect, your dad told you before your first day. There's a ladder. An order. You talk to the guy in charge, no matter what else anyone says. Lotta guys who think they know lotta things in the kitchen, but Chef's the only one who's not blowin' smoke up your ass.

"What do you need?" you say, rolling up your sleeves. When Zach's not around, Miguel is next in command. He's good, but you can tell he didn't go to culinary school. Everything I learn from Zach, he says.

You pull open the drawer and grab a chef's knife. You're not serious enough to bring your dad's old ones.

The kitchen is muggy. Miguel's eyes dart through the clouds. He puts a hand on his forehead. His nails are suspicious and long.

"I tired," he says. He's salary. Salary guys, like him, like Zach, work seventy-hour weeks. Sometimes, Miguel will say, no day off. He yawns. "I'm good, baby, you check Steph?"

"Not yet."

"You help. You good help. Thank you, baby." He touches your shoulder and aims his grin at your cheek. "Help Steph. She slow."

#

"Aioli, done. Shrimp purses, done. Brie-pear, done. Short ribs, done. Gnocchi, yeah," says Steph. Even her handwriting is tubby. She's one of those girls who likes to see herself print.

"Lamb," she says. "You good with that, JoAnimal?"

"Yeah." You pull out your phone, tell yourself you're checking that it's silenced just to check the messages, and set your disappointment on the shelf.

Lamb you grabbed from the freezer yesterday; lamb is unthawing in #5, the meat cooler, behind Zach's office. You yank through the suction to open the door and push away the strips of plastic curtaining the walk-in. The iron unctuousness of organs, bones, bleeding. Boxes of chicken thighs and steaks and uncoiled sausages, seared tenderloins and withering bacon, gray-scaled tilapia fillets; lamb comes two racks to a plastic-wrapped package, and eighteen bundles are unthawing in a pool of watery blood on a sheet tray.

Ever since Oliver told you about Zach hooking up with waitresses around the building, you've been waiting. You linger in walk-ins and shiver in freezers. You ponder dry storage, ignoring what's right in front of your face. Where are the wasabi sesame seeds, you ask yourself, heart racing, staring at them, six bottles of them, right there, next to the black sesame seeds, the white sesame seeds, the plum, the garlic. When will he pick you? You dawdle in the bakery, through the restaurant kitchen, a whole other entity from Zach's banquet-side domain, a downstairs connected to the locker room basement through old tunnels and molded-shut doors, and sneak handfuls of chocolate chips when you run to fetch dinner rolls. You're ready to get caught.

You hear the cooler door open and pause. Dwayne squints as he brushes aside the plastic curtain.

"You comin' out?" he says. You smell coffee on his breath. He takes his sugary, milky, which grosses you out. So milky, it's almost milk. You're a little afraid. You are what you eat, etc. He is sweet, creamy, hot liquid, guzzled. He has silvery white hair and a beard. A red face. A good smile, which you saw the residue of when you checked the registry and, under your sheets, your dad sleeping in the next room, were confronted with Dwayne's mug shot. He looks like Santa Claus, which is a way the universe messed up.

"Hellooo? Anyone in there?" he says. His voice is deep. "JoAnimal?"

You heft the sheet tray onto your shoulder, tighten your stomach to balance so you don't spill blood.

Dwayne backs through the plastic. "I'm trying to hold the door."

#

Things you wish you could forget: Dwayne's banana bread is one of them.

A weekend when you weren't working brunch. Brunch means Zach has you make breakfast bread pudding because he knows you like pastry; sometimes he even puts you on desserts for private dinners, lets you come into the kitchen on nights when there are no parties and prep, because he hates the Mansion bakery—everything is fake butter and three-letter shortening and vanillin and fruit cobbler biscuits that bake up raw. Nights you prepped for private dinners, you thought maybe you were reading the signs. Your Concord-grape focaccia was that good. Your espresso granita. Your pistachio biscotti. He was going to wait with you. Work side by side on something. Push you up against the grill. Burn your back.

Your brunch bread pudding is so ooey-good that once a server ran back to you with a pen and paper because a guest wanted the recipe.

This one day you weren't on brunch, so Dwayne made the bread pudding. Watch out JoAnimal, he said, when you showed up. I'm coming after your job.

What would this man have to do to become self-conscious about his threat potential?

What kind did you make? you said.

Dwayne grinned like a guy at a bar watching two girls make out.

Banana bread.

You nodded.

I make really good banana bread.

Nice, you said. Banana bread was the one thing your mom could make. Seventies food, she called it. She gave you that if you had to bring treats for school.

I make a great banana bread, Dwayne said. But my god-damn cat likes it.

You laughed.

He likes it so much, the other day I was home—I'd made some. And I sat down with a big glass of milk and a nice warm slice of banana bread. So I'm watching TV, and the cat comes over and bends down, and the little guy's got his pink tongue out, and what do you know, he's going to town on my banana bread! So I grab his neck and stick his face in the bread and hold him there, you know, and really let him know what he did wrong. 'NO. That's not for you. You don't touch my banana bread. Bad kitty!' His little face was all messed up. But you know—. Dwayne shook his head, shocked and proud.

#

In the calm before parties, your feeling is charitable-good. You love, for instance, Miguel's accent, which makes upstairs sound like oh-p-stairs. You love how Snoop and the other-garde-manger guy, Lee, guzzle coconut-nectar-pineapple-juice smoothies. You love that Zach doesn't end a text with a period, like your messages might never need to stop. You love how you've committed to Mountain Dew, an at-work ritual, thus sacred. Ceremonious. Like you're cementing your nostalgia for this time and place forever, once this time and place are over. The best thing about Mountain Dew is pouring it over ice in a plastic deli quart container. White Out bubbles like funky mineral water and fizzes tiny fireworks above the rim. Arctic Burst. Before you sip is the ultimate. Before sweetness and invisible caffeine. When the Mountain Dew is a cold calculation: two bottles equals under six hundred.

Growing up, your mom banned soda and white stuff: white sugar, white flour, white potatoes, white rice. She sprouted spelt and ate it with chopsticks. She presoaked oats. College was when you started sneaking, but now you're a slut for sugar. You just limit how much you need. Your father could never eat after being in the kitchen, and these days neither can you.

Before your crush, once you asked Zach: Don't you get hungry?

Who's got time for that? he said. Coffee pretty much shuts my stomach up.

You take a sip. Mountain Dew hurts your teeth and your tongue. All the colors taste the same: sweet, blunt, thought-muffling.

#

A fifty-person luncheon means three round plates of sesame chicken. Two squares of lamb. Two rectangles of shrimp shumai, stuck in pineapple hoisin.

How do you make that, you asked Oliver in the back-in-the-day days of the beginning.

You go to dry storage, he said, narrowing his eyes, looking like a very concentrated penis. You get a five-can of hoisin. You open it up, dump it in one of these. Whack up a pineapple and hit it with the stick.

The stick: an immersion blender as tall as your calf. The plastic container of hoisin and pineapple wiggles with the vibrations, and you have to steady it between your feet while you squeeze the motor, and the blender roars in your grip. If Oliver's working, he snickers until you tell him to shut up and then he lifts his dark eyebrows up his pale pink forehead and fake focuses on what he's doing, and you smile, but just with your mouth.

#

The first few months at the Mansion were ugly. You couldn't remember how to turn on the buffalo chopper or how to jimmy the robocoupe with a chopstick or where to find the blender. You wore regular gym shoes and slipped a lot, and the guys were like, Whoa, whoa, whoa, there she goes, is she—is she—she's okay! You wore the stupid skullcap. You were slow, you couldn't remember what went in which walk-in, you were afraid of making eye contact with anyone. Because what would they see? A girl playing tough. A girl who wanted to work herself into someone else.

During plating, when everyone gathered at the line to heap plates and pass them down and get covered with a plastic lid, there was the night Dwayne screamed at you for scooping mashed potatoes wrong.

Don't level it off every time, he said, standing across from you on the line, carving a bloody tube of meat.

Zach stood next to you, overseeing. You watched his arms. Was he touching your fingers on purpose when he passed you the plates? You stepped a stalk of celery closer to him. He was placing three spears of asparagus, tips pointing to twelve o'clock, between Dwayne's meat and your potatoes.

There were four hundred plates to scoop. You nodded, didn't think. You kept leveling.

What are you doing? Dwayne barked. I told you, quit it with those potatoes. This isn't a lunchroom. They look cheap.

#

Denial.

You threw down the scooper and faced the ovens.

What the hell are you doing? Dwayne asked. Sweat poured down his red face, and some kid who only lasted a few days oooh-ed.

I'm not doing anything, you said.

Honey, honey, Zach said. Get back on the line, and let's everyone calm down.

#

Anger.

You threw down the scoop.

Who do you think you are? you said to Dwayne. The kitchen stopped. Where do you get off telling me how to scoop? If they weren't supposed to be level, wouldn't I be using a goddamn spoon? My dad told me all about you, shitface, so don't you tell me that I'm doing it wrong.

#

Bargaining.

All right, Dwayne, you said, setting down the scoop. How about I carve the roast and you scoop the potatoes? If you let me cut the meat, I'll let you make these portions any way you want. I'll let you do potatoes.

#

Depression.

You threw down the scoop and ran down to the locker room.

Fuck this, fuck this, you thought. Six months at the Mansion was long enough. Respectable. You wished your dad would save you; you immediately took it back. He didn't need another woman with problems.

You sat on the bench, facing your stuff. You could leave. Drive back to the dorms. Someone would hide you out, and you could do another dirty job there.

You heard steps, running down by twos.

JoAnimal, Zach called.

Your stupid nickname. You chopped off the tip of your thumb making lobster salad and wouldn't let anyone call your dad to take you home. You worked through: that made you an animal.

He rounded the corner. Blue eyes. Golden-brown fade. He sat next to you, his thigh against your thigh.

Hey, he said, like a guy from your twentieth-century European history class. He didn't have something weird or criminal about him. He liked baseball and Cormac McCarthy novels. Maybe someday you would be this capable, capable/

responsible/together: Zach was only a few years older than you but in charge of a whole kitchen.

Dwayne's an asshole, all right? Zach said. He looked embarrassed. Your dad had to tell you that. Everyone's cranky by Saturday, but Dwayne—that fella's king.

You nodded. You blamed your mom: you missed her, and she knew you were going to miss her, and she was the one who kept ignoring her doctors, and you were the one who kept expecting things to change, and your dad was the one who kept pissing you off, but really he was just being a realist. She's on her own course, he said, a few days before she died. She was the one who passed out three times on the elliptical.

I'm sorry, you said, but it was only maybe your fault. For a moment, you were honest with yourself: you just wanted someone to tell you that you weren't all wrong.

He patted your knee and left his hand there. Up and down his arms, burns and scars and scabs were rashy, flushed from heat. This close, he looked reptilian.

#

"I'll scoot," Steph says. Estimating, you bet her hips are ten inches wider than yours.

"Can you just push over that garbage?"

"You got it."

From under the first dish pit, you grab a stack of sheet trays—wet and still greasy, soapy, even after the ice-pink sanitizer bath. Nothing at the Mansion ever feels clean.

Set the sheet trays over the mouth of the trash can. Knife the plastic packaging, pull out the lamb, discard the plastic, untangle the racks, place on the tray, repeat. Listen to Steph tell you about her boyfriend's sweet sneaker commission at Dick's. Drizzle the racks with olive oil and sprinkle them with salt and rough-chopped rosemary. Massage the meat and flip. Top sides up, they look like cave paintings of extinct mammals.

"Jooooo-Anna, Joooo-Anna," says Tito, the morning dishwasher. His baseball cap is flipped inside out. How does that even work? He clutches a plastic pitcher of fruit punch.

"Tee-toooh, Tee-toooh," you echo.

"Tee-toooh, Tee-toooh," he says back, spraying water into a sixty-gallon pot.

You heft the tray of lamb and head to the grill. Otherwise this will never end.

#

When the servers parade, it's time to get it in gear. You better have your station set up. You better have a hotel pan on a wet towel so the pan won't slip. Squeeze bottles of aioli and squeeze bottles of olive oil, sesame seeds for garnishing sesame chicken, chopped scallions, chiffonaded basil, minced parsley, edible orchids. Your Mountain Dew loaded with ice. Your hors d'oeuvres fired and ready and pushed to the front of the trays in the hotbox. Cocktail napkins fanned on trays. Flowers from centerpieces scattered on trays. Picks and silver mini-forks and silver mini-spoons and tiny porcelain plates and edible wafer cones.

"Your plates look the best," pig-nosed Val tells you, shaking her graying blond hair. She's the server manager, and she's in charge of assigning limp high school girls to butler-passed hors d'oeuvres. Even her boobs look fat. She's wearing a sleeveless satin blouse with a plunging neck, and you can see sweat beading her cleavage.

"The guys did it Sunday, and everything looked like shit."

"Have you seen Zach?" you say, arranging bacon-wrapped scallops on a bed of arugula.

When she chews, her mouth puffs like a bellows. She shakes her head.

"Mhmnm," she says, swallowing. You see the wad go down her throat. "No."

#

You hate Val for at least three reasons:
1) On the cardboard tents she prints out for the trays, she spells phyllo "pilo."
2) She picks sticky nuggets of sesame chicken right from your box.
3) Zach.

#

Maybe you're only telling yourself today feels different so that today will feel different. By the end of the luncheon, the first Mountain Dew is gone.

"I made you a plate," says Steph. "You need help?"

"I'm good," you say. "Take a break." When she goes out to sit on the milk crates, you scrape the food into the trash.

You test yourself: are these shallot tears or real tears? You are glad you gave up mascara.

#

It isn't a shift without imagining yourself bold.

Party over, you find him in his office cube, across from the line, reviewing tomorrow's schedule. He's any guy staring at his Mac. His chef coat is unbuttoned.

You knock on the window, even though the door's open.

Hey, he says, and his voice isn't yelling or instructing but already listening to you. Focused.

Do you want to smoke? you say, swallowing your pulse.

He feels for the pack in his pants. He looks at you.

Give me five.

You're face-to-face behind the building; you're leaning on the kitchen, and Zach's leaning on the fence. Gravel and cigarette butts beneath your feet. Mosquitos flock to the floodlight that spills on the bucket shed. You lean back, your legs out in front of you. You can see his pecs through his T-shirt. V-neck, matted blond chest hair. He slouches and surveys the ground, but then he looks up, his mouth a serious yes.

Inside everyone is no one, a bunch of guys smearing soap with tangled-steel scrubbers on the tables and ovens and stoves and grills and hotboxes. Others following with towels. Not you. Not Zach.

You're stubbing out your cigarette when he asks you what you're doing. What your plans are. He doesn't ask about your dad. You say something great: you say, I'm planning to ask you to go for a drink.

He laughs. Smooth, JoAnimal.

You get in his truck. He drives you across the river.

Where are we going? you ask.

He keeps driving. He plays jazz. He's not talking.

You live here? you say. He parks in front of the yellow house. The mound of trash still towers, garbage in the dark. Inside the rooms are Mansion ugly. Mauve carpet.

When he peels off his white T-shirt, his body is covered with red scales and scabs.

He presses your face into the turquoise couch.

When he touches you, you pass out. He sets you in bed. He sets you in the bed of his truck. He gets you a Queen bed at the inn. He drives you to the foot of a mountain and wakes you, feeding you ice chips from a Styrofoam cup.

#

You put down your knife and check your phone. Your dad: I love you always. Extra today.

You picture him: swiping a dirt-worn finger across the glass of the fish tank, trying to make the catfish vacuum up the algae; adjusting the band on the basketball shorts he still wears even though he hasn't played pick-up at the gym in years; checking the clock—2:35 p.m.—and what are the odds he never remembers what time he was born, and he'll always remember what time his wife died?

#

"Smoke one?" Miguel says, halfway to your station. You wipe your shallot tears with your sleeve and grab your phone. Text your dad: Want me to come home?

You don't really smoke, but you like to hold a cigarette and listen to men talk while one burns between your fingers. Miguel leads you behind the building, over the stones and the pipes and the generator, to where the gazebos paths split leading down to the river.

He holds out a tired fist.

Pound.

"Boom city," he says, with a wan smile.

"La ciudad de boom," you say.

You exhale menthol. You're uneven; there's breaded chicken smashed on your shoe.

"I tired," he says. "Can you help me, JoAní?"

The sun leaks through the clouds, bluing the sky. Everything looks greener against the approaching dim.

"I still haven't seen Zach," you say. You scrape the bottom of your shoe on the ground. There are days you can't get through and days you will yourself to become capable. "Is it supposed to storm?"

"No sé," says Miguel. "Why? You wanna go home?"

#

Acceptance

You threw down the scoop. One-in-ten were your mother's odds. Those I'll take, she said. Heart attack: one-in-three? Cancer: one-in-two? Just don't bet against me—or bury me. I want to be burned.

At the end, you could fit your purse inside the gap between her thighs. At the end, her skin was dishrag gray and baby-puppy furred. Her breathing was stitches, ripped up and ripped up and ripped out, the hem of her undone. Her heart was a moldy prune. At the end, you felt fat at her funeral. You walked out the kitchen door without gathering your things. You sat on a milk crate. No one joined you. No one touched your thigh. You were in the kitchen one minute, and the next you were gone.

Cake Eater

I stared and the man ate. Cake in his grip, he reminded me of a cartoon bear pawing honey. He had round eyes as white as frosting. He stood at the end of the bar, where the cake was set out next to a caddy of garnishes, limes and lemons and cocktail onions, on a gold board with scalloped edges—a sheet cake commemorating an event someone had forgotten to celebrate. Really, when is cake mere compliment?

The man had a globular stomach and held the cake like a sandwich. I was fascinated, horrified, and already aroused: I had never seen an adult eat cake in this manner. Before I could second-guess myself, I was walking up to him. Closer, I could see the wrinkles in his shirt. That made sense. His pants didn't: dark denim that I knew could ink one's thighs.

"Hey—" I pointed to the cake in his hand, the piece on my plate. "Is it worth it?"

He chewed as much as you need to with soft cake goodly iced. His gaze swabbed my face, the way my doctor mined my cervix.

"Not bad," he said. "Though it's no breast milk."

I was amused but used to louche fellows, true reproachables. This man had a jutting quality, like he was being yanked forward, off a shelf. I focused my vision on his porous forehead. My cake stiffened.

"You're a father then," I said.

"Twins," the man said. "Patty cake, patty cake."

"You have your hands full."

"But with what?" At that, he squeezed the cake in his grip. The frosting squelched—it would've been a sound we heard if the music weren't loud, a falsetto chanting: "Afraid to die."

The man clearly meant this desecration to punctuate our exchange, but I was alone, pregnant, and desperate to be defiled, so I followed him outside. We found ourselves standing at a tall table in the plastic bubble blistered over the front of the building. Call it a tent, but there were many windows and a roof with fans, the blades molded to resemble bamboo, slowly rustling the humectant air.

"I have to ask you: Why exactly are you at this event?" the man said.

"A favor, a past," I said. "More or less, a reunion. Before I give birth."

"I didn't recognize you!" he said suddenly. "Now I see. Your arms are different."

"We barely know each other then," I said. "But now we both like cake."

The windows in the plastic enclosing us were opaque with exhalation. I nudged the cake around my plate, using the chin of the fork. I had only raked the frosting.

The man ate his last bite and smiled. "The frosting is homeless shelter frosting. Food pantry frosting. ¿Te hablas español?"

I did speak Spanish, I hola-ed to everyone in my neighborhood, but I couldn't come up with a claro, por supuesto, cómo no. I balanced the cake on my belly. What of it, getting dirty, sucia? Sticky sweat was glomming my camisa, where the cotton clung to my spine. My newly popped navel pressed against the cloth like a spare button.

"Let me tell you: it's not as hard as you think," the man said. "I was very energized by fatherhood, and my wife is wonderful with directions. Giving them. She's a project manager for a stable. From farm to table? How about from pasture to Saratoga?"

"Your children will ride?" I said, hoping to sound suggestive.

"God, no, please no," the man said. He wiped his hands on his shirt, where they left a crumbly white smudge like dead skin. "We're horse-eating people. From the north."

Somewhere in the night, there was a sound, like the exoskeleton of Earth's core being crunched. I was nervous, but one gets nothing as the instigator of fear—not without smoke or fireworks. There's a gulf between fear and nervousness, pain and lonesomeness, anger and solitude. The man was keeping me company. He might come back to my hotel, down for a discalced romp, parenthetical, unthinkable. He had pink on his lip from a lone frosting rose.

"You want to see something straight awesome?" the man said.

I shrugged, but lord was I ever: desperate, desperate, desperate. I left my cake on the table.

He pushed out the tent and into the barking night. I

followed him up the footpath, through a grove of bare magnolias, and into the parking lot. I was still hungry, and the baby was turning, glowing, worming. I had seen others eating cake from waxy cups, the tiny breed that comes with water coolers. I regretted not smashing mine into one of those.

The man reached into the tight back pocket of his dark denim and pinched some remote. This was his car: the Carrera irradiated inside by green flashing lights. He nodded at the illumination, perhaps expecting a remark on the color, but I had my own father whose convertible could strobe, interiorly, exteriorly, with a dial's twist. I had a husband, too, some other fuckery.

"Meet the mother of my children," he said. "And the twins. Cula and Carl."

He opened the back door on the driver's side and stepped aside. A crimp-coated cocker spaniel panted there, lying on a pillow inlaid with silvery rope. It shone in an emerald tremor of overhead lights. There were two friendly faced stuffed baby dolls in the dog's nest and a spear of bone, elk antler, most likely.

I wanted to go. I had the room nearby, a room from whence I had wandered in search of a convincing meal, conversation, some belittled cumming. I had kept my heart as open as batter for eggs. Now the humidity was mounting. My uterus was cramping. The hailstorm forecasted had never broke. I had counted on weather to relieve my problems, but the weather was a coward. Like me.

"You see, without a witness, this is nothing," the man said, unbuttoning his shirt. He crouched as though he were fetching items from a very low shelf in the grocery. In the green overhead dim, the sparse hair on his chest was whiskery, wiry, feelers on a microscopic bug.

The cocker spaniel rolled over and exposed her scrubbed belly, nipply and speckled. The man picked up the baby dolls, roughly, much as he had picked up the cake, and situated them near the dog's heart. Between a Y of blue veins, I swear, I could see a tremulous pulse.

By now the night was burned up and starving. I took a few steps back.

"My father, my father," the dog barked.

"My darling, my darling," the man said, and his face grew compassionate, and he knelt on the seat and set a hand on the lower abdomen of the dog.

I imagined the cake back in my hand. I imagined stabbing the cake and taking a bite. It was marble. The chocolate was indistinct from the vanilla cloaked in all that icing. Roseless, sugarful, stupid cake. I expected such cake for a push present.

"Do you need a nurse or a midwife?" I said.

The man looked at me, puzzled. By that time, he was fully inside his own back seat and, with one of his hind legs, he kicked the door.

Soon it was noisy with suckling and his windows began to fog. There was cake smeared on the front of my camisa, and I walked back to my hotel, watching my shadow grow rounder and rounder until it was a shadow globe.

Alone in bed: my stomach howled, I opened my legs. In the next room, a dog yapped like a snapping wet rag. Could he smell me, my hormonal torte, so progesterone? Whatever the odor, I was embarrassed and yet more defiant than usual. Perhaps I was great with child, but there was no way I could wait until breakfast.

Lisa Is the Water

"The worst toy for a bulimic is a garbage disposal," you say.

Saturday afternoon on the balcony, flattened out in bikinis with pink rosettes kissing the waist, glasses of Perrier and a bowl of limes on the towel between you and Lisa. Summer physics ended yesterday, and you've been fasting since the final to be angles and elbows for back-to-school.

Lisa flips. Her blond hair drips down her back, and her shoulder blades jut like wings.

"No way," Lisa says. "All-you-can-eat buffet."

"You're cliché," you say. "Everyone says that."

"Who's everyone?"

"Every girl in every hospital." You think Lisa may be getting a little dippy, to lift one of your mother's favorites. All that time she's spending with Chris: Semen kills brain cells. You're a little light-headed evaluating the situation through sunglasses, trying to clench your transverse abdominals, peeved, like when you clogged the drain in the bathtub and needed to pour a whole Drano down and didn't want to call your father to get the window—that was last month. Always with those windows that stick. Why are they so hard to open?

The fast is new; the season, the same. You and Lisa have committed to summer school to rid yourselves of requirements, but you've never seen Lisa let a boy eat up so much of her time. Before you were high schoolers, you sat next to each other in a chilly lab relearning home row and business letter blocks. And chemistry: you burned peanuts and calculated a calorie—nothing but energy enough to heat one measly gram of water.

Now you picture yourself in the white lab coat you borrowed from the teacher every day; that summer you were so cold, you called your hands prayer candles.

Mottled, lit, blue.

Half a day you laze away while maintenance buzzes below. Big green trucks from Crown Disposal stink gasoline across the lawn and snatch grass from the cul-de-sac; men prune and trim, roses and hedges. Beneath your balcony, a crew of gray jumpsuits tends to a bed of impatiens with handhelds like weaponry, engines revving—eight men, burnished and sweating.

"I think we should be done," you say. "I'm really . . . from the sun." At the gym, you almost passed out during spinal imprints. Long legs, the instructor crowed through her puffy bangs. Remember your powerhouse, ladies. Pilates is what stays still!

"Dizzy."

"You don't feel good? I feel totally good, just like . . . chill," Lisa says. She props herself on her elbows, wipes a hair from her forehead. Picks up a lime and dunks it in her sparkling water. Sucking the fruit lights her eyes. "Mmm, do this. Fizzy."

You glare at your watch.

"We're not eating until five." You move the band up your elbow and lust on the bracelet of pale flesh, the sweat-plastered, brindle-brown hair. If you were alone, you'd nose the skin, inhale animal and wood chips and sun. "It's quarter after two."

Your body leaves a long, dark oval on the towel when you sit and reach for your robe. Coward. Viscera of soul. You avoid your stomach: bending forward or reaching down or craning for the alarm or right after you've eaten—fine, all food bloats your belly just the same; when you stare yourself down in the mirror, you think you'd be fine—for a pregnant bitch.

"It's a lime," Lisa says. She cracks her neck. Tendons, striae, pretty, slack. "Ten calories."

You stare. Lower your voice: "So, what else doesn't count?"

Lisa's face shrinks, a sucked-out prune. "Nothing, nothing else—all right? Re-lax. I just think the point of the fast is to not eat. A lime's not really, like, eating."

"I'd say ten calories is like . . . eating," you say.

Mocking you learned from your mother. Smog in air. Nothing but summer. It's you and Lisa. So Lisa's not your best friend anymore, no problem. Maybe she can collect your assignments when you head back to the hospital.

"It doesn't matter," you say. You imagine displacing the blood racing through your body with bubbling water until you feel nothing, maybe benevolent, mostly dizzy. Breathe in: blood pressure tumble. Out: wafting neurotrauma. No one's making you eat a stupid lime.

#

Lisa slips into the bedroom, past your vanity, all clothing and charts, your diaries, one for tracking and another, blank, waiting for recovery to clutch your stupid shoulders and douse you with fat. She grabs her clothes from the back of a chair and disappears into the bathroom to change while you wait.

You're alone in your bedroom. You're so ethereal from fasting, you want to wear something with a skirt to usher air in and out, but all your dresses look like they're waiting for someone else. A silhouette better than yours.

Lisa.

Reframe, reframe, reframe—so, okay, maybe there's no such thing as better.

Loose in the bust, looser in the hips, scoop-necked and white. Who will judge if your swimsuit shows through? You're your only judge. The halter brands your neck, a floppy bow tipped with shiny gold charms.

You sit on your bed and stare at the television, mute. Scoot to the edge. A million music video countdowns, junk food, and trash. No wonder your parents tried the cable ban: Kurt Cobain is lambent; cheerleaders' braids are swinging; a crowd swells; a janitor mopes with his bucket.

"Wanna go to the mall?" you say.

You picture Lisa on the other side of the door.

Legs: scalpels, ice picks, bone. Bone and more bone, nuzzled under Lisa's golden, sun-kissed flesh. Nothing hungry in her eyes. Breasts: plump. Bouncy, even. What would she do with your mouth?

"The mall is freezing."

"It's like a hundred degrees out," you say, swiping a finger behind your knee where sweat gathers in a thin stripe like the moistened seal of an envelope. Barely a secret. You're overheating and Lisa's freezing?

No way Lisa is thinner.

"I'm sick of shopping," Lisa says. "Let's go to the V."

#

You don't just suspect this has a lot to do with Chris; the V means Chris, head lifeguard who keeps Lisa at the pool late, way after close, to kiss her long ballerina neck beneath a sky blistered with stars. This is your favorite way to think of Lisa—though you've heard about hot tub parties, flirty drinking games and fingerprint bruises—no, not jealousy. Envy you buy at a counter. Lisa's always inviting you, calling you, offering to pick you up or bring you out, but you're convinced your parents just pay Lisa to help you maintain normal teenage life—like they know you that well, like they get that you'd rather be studying your ascetic saints than cruising the cul-de-sac with Lisa; that, every night, you wrestle yourself into believing that God will cradle your consciousness like a worry stone when you finally win, with a clavicle gnash and your pulse's ultimate curlicue, when you wear your body down.

#

The matching halter strap around Lisa's neck? One velum valentine after another floats through your body, your heart shaved on a mandoline. Your breath quickens; your stomach growls: inside, another continent, where everything graspable drowns.

Lisa stops a foot from the television and gapes. Kurt Cobain's twine-y hair slaps his forehead; her face is still pink blushed, flushed.

"He was so hot—so hot, such a freak. . . ."

43

"You tell me," you say. "Where are we going?"

Stanch your want with gravel, sand, clay, dirt.

"The V, yeah? Chris is working." She pulls her pinky across her teeth. "We get stuff free."

#

Lisa drives to the pool listening to a station playing upbeat pop. Top down, windows down, air conditioning blasting your feet. Pool bags in the back seat. In yours—towel, sunblock, a roll of Necco wafers to ease you from the fast. What's inside Lisa's tote?

You look at your nails, try to rename the polish. Appointments. You have these. You have, also, a manicurist. Trainer, nutritionist, doctor, shrink. Who else do you see other than Lisa and your parents, the cook and the landscapers, the men who occupy the gatehouse? When was the last time you even went to the pool? All you remember is your final summer with the diving team, a few months before your twelfth birthday—normal as ever, when you did a one-and-a-half and slammed into the ice-blue board. Three rectangular gouges: forehead, chin, the bridge of your nose.

Charred meat and lilacs. Suburban trap of traffic and stop signs. Lisa sings along to every single song and some jingles. When the light turns red, Lisa stops too close. You turn into your mother: gasp and shrink, pump an imaginary brake. And if there's a man in the car on Lisa's side, she lowers her heart-shaped sunglasses and looks. Bats her eyes, licks her lips, hi.

"You do it," she says. "C'mon."

"I'm not flirting with some old man, Lisa."

"Make his dreams come true," she says. "Every father wants a sixteen-year-old."

"Sick," you say. "Nausea."

Three dreams. Your father: dead; your mother: banished. You unbuckle your nerdy chemistry teacher's belt with your teeth. Wake up and wait for your wanting to quit.

"Okay, look," Lisa says. "Red bug, on your right." She glances and, from behind your glasses, you follow her eyes. He's wearing a white tank top and aviators, gold. "Oh my god, those arms."

"Are you hungry?" you say. Lamb-spit arms. Chainsaw guns.

"No. Remember? That lime?" She reaches over and swats your wrist. "Kidding."

"No," you say. He's drumming the steering wheel to blaring dance music, and you wish you could apologize for catching him in such a pathetic pose.

"Seriously, if you don't, I will," Lisa says. "Do it." Sun sparks her lips. Her mouth is one fat wish. "Do it—the light's about to change."

"No."

Lisa cranks the radio and he turns. "Now!"

You don't think. You pivot in your seat, little smile, wave. His eyebrows appear over the top of his glasses. He grins: perfect canines.

And green, zoom, onward, he's gone.

Lisa eyes you, her mouth open wide—a gob of neon gum and her silver filling (second molar, lower left). She laughs and throws her hands up, accelerating past the park district.

"Now, what about that was so bad?"

#

45

By the time you reach the pool, you're picking off your polish. Trying to flick it between the door and the seat. There's not much to get excited about when therapy teaches you how to manage all your epiphanies. And Lisa gets out of the car, yawns, and stretches her long, thin arms above her head. You've never seen any drastic weight changes—in fact, Lisa's always been slender—now she's just grown into it like a starlet—and, here she is, fasting for fun. Poor Lisa, you think. She got gorgeous; she got lazy.

"What are you going to eat first?" Lisa crouches, reapplying her lip gloss and pouting in the side mirror. "I feel so gross, but I know I want a pretzel. Or, like, frozen pizza—you know? Or, sickest—oh, I'm nasty: Chris has me hooked on churros in cheese."

Your decision is instant.

"I'm extending," you say. Catherine of Siena ate flesh and herbs; Beatrice bound herself with cords. For the first time in weeks, you feel your devotion ticking.

"Till tomorrow."

"I don't really think that's a good idea. . . ." Lisa says, but you're already walking to the gate.

The V is tucked away behind a grove of weeping willows. The parking lot is a wash of gravel, a couple basketball hoops near the fence that wraps around the pool. A picnic pavilion with benches and grills, a bulletin board behind glass where swim practice schedules are posted along with Swimmers of the Week. From the lot, you hear screams, splashing, music tinny over the loudspeaker—everything in the distance glistening and candy. As you walk, small stones crack like teeth against the soles of your sandals.

Lisa jogs over in her sequined flip-flops, her tote banging against her hip, electric tangerine. Is the rubber strap digging pink into her shoulder? Water, aloe, neon gel: a salve for any sore. She catches up with you before the locker room.

"Would you wait, or are you going to be a bitch the rest of the day?"

"I'm not a bitch," you say, letting your own bag dangle off your wrist. You put your hand on your hip, thumb the bone, breathe in, glance at Lisa, and look down. You've gotten good at shaking away her face.

"How am I a bitch?"

Two boys in saggy trunks and mesh water shoes tear past, through the beds of red geraniums that line the sidewalk up to the front desk. "You're it," one of them screams, pointing at you and jogging backwards before he disappears.

"Hon," Lisa says. "Can I give you a hug?"

Brace yourself. Hugs happen whether you like them or not. Lisa's a few inches taller than you, and when she hugs you it's not two clanging skeletons—Lisa's breasts press into your chest. Things you don't have. Her hands rub your back. Hip bones, spine, the fine hairs glistening above her lip. You're drowsy off contact.

Up close, Lisa smells like ice cream, coconut.

Up close, you peer, finally, into her bag: towel; lightweight novel; a bag of pink-frosted animal crackers; a blue condom wrapper.

You pull away, tuck your hair behind your ears, stare hard, and try to say something, not just anything.

"It's not good to full-on fast," Lisa says. "You told me that."

"I know."

"So, stop at five. Like the plan."

"I don't really want to," you say, licking your lower lip, tasting your skin, dark as blood blisters.

"Chris will give us food. At least get a Diet Coke."

"I'm fine. I just need a swim."

#

You take five minutes peeing so you don't have to rinse off in the communal shower. You've seen it before: water beads Lisa's forehead like a veil; droplets cling to Lisa's nose like fleet piercings. When you're sure she's gone, you're alone in the steam. There are no mirrors, no curtains, no cover for tears. The water pelts your back. The floor tires your feet.

Lisa is on deck, beneath the guard's chair where Chris scans the diving well. Chris can give her food. Lisa is so aimless; Lisa needs to eat. You settle between a woman asleep in a black one-piece and an old man with breasts like soft triangles. You spread your towel out and sit down; you rifle through your bag until you find sunblock. From here, Chris is a bright blue nose and sunglasses, tousled honey hair, and a runner's concave chest. Rarely do you admit to yourself: you're so hungry that you're not. You're so hungry, when you rest a hand on the slats of the chair, you watch your fingers float off, one by one, lifting toward Lisa. And Chris is twirling his whistle. Chris, who feeds her. And the woman in the black suit snores. The old man clears his throat. You squirt lotion onto your palm and feel your face. Ridge of nose, plum-skin eyes, stupid mouth. The line up the high dive is deep.

#

When will you find yourself at the V again?

Each summer will be less Lisa than the last.

Each summer: another step away from turning back.

Two more summers: independence. Three? Four? Five? A lustrum? The freedom of choosing when and how to end.

#

Your turn to climb the ladder. You grip each rung tight and just feel, just deal, bear it; it makes you want to vomit: the sloughed-off skin of other people's feet, the moisture clinging to the metal, and then, at the top, that dirty plank. So, you think, okay, two minutes; give yourself two minutes because bodies have amassed, queued, and you're not even nearing the edge. Just think about it. Just think. Just your friend and a thin slice of skin on her back, what the strap leaves light, and the rest of her body—soft caramel—and the tuft of hair between her legs sequined with saliva, so it's Lisa and Lisa, just Lisa. Lisa in the water, Lisa in the kiddie pool, Lisa inflating dolphins, Lisa your flotation device, Lisa licking, it's too slippery, Lisa saying, Well yah I said yea when he, as in ohyea, like ohyesbaby, Lisa in a car pinkying Xs and Os, Lisa as your mirror, Lisa's hands and knees—it's no biggie, whatever, Lisa in the shower, Lisa skipping class, Lisa in the hot tub in her basement, above ground in the dark, Lisa and the Coke can, Lisa and the lights, all night Lisa, and the handcuffs tight, Lisa and the what, so I liked it, Lisa and donuts or batteries, melon!, Lisa drinking tons of water and fuck, nails Pacific Blue, picking out a pearl thong, purchasing the Pleasure Pack, Lisa in the future, Lisa with a football player, Lisa horizontal, Lisa saying multiple, we're talking three or four, holy holy fuck, Lisa Jesus Christing through getting eaten out, Lisa and her ankles, Lisa to the wall, Lisa on all fours, Lisa on her back on her front with her legs straight in a V two fingers on her lips with her tongue touching her chin with her eyelashes with her hair with her stomach sticky and flattened and toned and teased: parenthesis.

The whistle blows.

Chris points from his perch. His neck is bruised. Lisa.

Inhale and swallow. Your saliva tastes like beeswax. You turn around. Walking off means backing down the ladder or a peerless concrete drop. Your heart's pounding; your stomach's stinging; you grip the rails and feel for the rung, your gut level with the board.

And you smell her: Coconut. Sun-soaked hair. Candy-sweet wrists.

"Babe!" she yells.

You look down: nothing but Lisa, kiss-pink lips eating up the sun.

The Scar

I have a friend who has always been thin. Both Sasha's parents, well into their fifties, are lanky, and, for as long as I have known Sasha—since our earliest years of schooling—her parents have been this way, pale academics whom I now see were out of place in the southwest suburbs of Chicago where we were raised. Though Sasha has long moved away, I assume her whole family remains thin. Sasha's mother, Anna, would sweat nights on a rowing machine in their basement; for her constitution, she subscribed to walks around the neighborhood where they lived and still live today.

Removed from the subdivision hubs by a road that leads straight into the endless deciduous Orland forests, my friend's family had settled apart from cul-de-sacs and gated communities to live closer to Sasha's mother's father, a doctor who practiced out of his home. As children, Sasha and I would invade this property as if it were our own. The Doctor and his wife, a tawny woman named Myrna, would frequently drive north to their Sun Prairie farm, and Sasha and I would be unleashed to visit the Doctor and Myrna's large dogs, eat ice cream sitting on the counters in the wood-paneled kitchen, and sink into the rooftop hot tub we accessed by climbing a vertical ladder in an upstairs guest room's closet. We spent one New Year's Eve in the Doctor's massage room, lying on leather-covered tables while young boyfriends kneaded our backs, chopping, working out love knots with their mouths.

Youth—all those rooms with clear designations: two bedrooms, a well-upholstered living room, a piano parlor; a sunroom where, come spring, we watched the backyard pink; the grandfather's den of bookshelves crammed with medical texts; and a hallway door that led to the office, where patients were seen.

Upon entering the office, we would invade a supply room: tongue depressors and hypodermic needles, speculums in noisy paper and, in glass jars, gauze swabs like cotton candy. On the opposite side of the hallway, the single hallway (for this was a small office) was the receptionist's pen: swiveling chair, printer with plastic shield that spat paper with perforated margins, two walls of jelly-bright files. Years later, another doctor would join Sasha's grandfather's practice, and my own family would visit that doctor for all varieties of ailments, but, when we were wandering that hallway, the examining rooms were unexpected and dim. I say "dim" for it was always night when we came by, and, despite now having seen those rooms many more times in daylight, my own self reclined on the chatty parchment, when I imagine the doctor's office, it is always night. A fat circle of a light on a bendable neck, the burgundy examining tables, paintings of lighthouses illuminating boats crashing at sea. The tools locked in their sterile envelopes. The scales, stalky beasts, black and cold; the noise as you step on the coarse platform, adjust the iron balancers, wrenches the silence.

It was not uncommon for Sasha and me to visit the office during sleepovers. As we grew older and our friendship loosened to include other girls, we almost certainly spent some portion of the night moving through the dark. And these nights of creeping around another person's house, after viewing some movie or other we wouldn't feel comfortable watching with the threat of parents, dosed us with small freedoms and dangers, as I understand now, for we might anonymously dial boys or raid a blameless fridge or simply make noise long after adults were likely to retire, even though Sasha's parents were never parents who chided us for remaining awake. The truth? Sasha's parents were the only parents I knew who were hands-off, more concerned with their own lives than ours. Sasha's mother was a minor Douglas Sirk scholar who taught at a private high school on the North Side, and Sasha's father, once a Latin teacher, preached at a mysterious organization whose mission was to dissuade teenagers from experimenting with drugs. Sasha's father was a bald-headed expert, a snarky man in wire-framed glasses who looked like a monk. Before he'd married Sasha's mother, he had produced two daughters, who, as far as I could tell, had achieved little. They both lived with their mother in Minnesota—three women working as bank tellers. On the other hand, Sasha's mother had been married before with spectacular results. Andrew, her son from her first marriage, was handsome when I knew him, sixteen to our eight, and, to this day, has only grown more so; he attended a liberal arts college and then medical school, gracing his arm with an old-money Manhattanite named Esther whom he met over a cadaver and married twice, at two ceremonies: one in New York and one in Chicago. But Sasha was the only child her parents had together produced, and the shadowy and older presences of these half-siblings reared her into a strange and unsettling child.

During second grade, before we became friends, Sasha and I participated in a course for high-achieving children. We were labeled *gifted*, and as gifted students, we would be excused from *SSR*, or silent sustained reading, and escorted to a mobile classroom in the school's backyard. These classrooms were in trailers, and it was nearly high school before I connected *mobile*, as in our *mobile* classroom, and *mobile*, as in *mobile home*. As a teenager, I developed an extreme distaste for the quality of mobility in a residence, though not related to any particular circumstances that would befall me or my family; it was just that I developed a fear of trailers. And this distaste did not diminish when I learned that Sasha's handsome half brother, Andrew, had grown up in a trailer before Sasha was born. No, thereupon, I could not help but regard the family as plagued by some irreversible trailer-life curse. This curse extended onto Sasha and Sasha's father and even Sasha's half sisters and their nameless, shapeless mother. Even their banks were cursed. Still, I never spoke these feelings to Sasha, or to anyone for that matter, not even the girls we allowed into our friendship during high school, though I had been told this information neither in coven nor confidence.

On many occasions, Sasha would reveal something to me. Secrets. As one of those children who seemed to collect damage, a sort of precious misfortune, Sasha would regale me with one trauma or another that I understood was not to be shared. Not with our lesser friends, not with my parents; not with priests or the adults who gavaged our religious education; not with doctors or counselors or teachers. These people—adults—I maintain, to this day, would not have known what to do with the information Sasha disclosed. All of it was green. When Sasha and I climbed on top of the lockers in the girls' locker room, nobody could have understood more clearly what Sasha was telling me than me. For what she shared became mine: Her father underwent a vasectomy. She was allergic to guava juice. Her mother told her that it was all right if she collected flick knives. Sasha's brother, Andrew, asked her to model a series of secondhand peignoirs for him and ranked them on a scale of 1 to 7. The secrets of our young lives. I became her.

Just as easily, I might have found her manner unpersuasive, the details too gruesome. When I first met her in second grade, I was not charmed. In the mobile classroom where we gifted students were gathered, Sasha stuck out, tiny and elfin with dark brown bangs, which, rather than having been cut straight across, seemed to be longer above her nose, shaggily tapering into a point. She wore turtlenecks, and she reminded me of a bat. Possibly, she expressed a tomboyish interest in bats; there was another member of our cohort, a gamesome boy named Ian, who also had uncomfortable brown hair and, without a doubt, an expressed adoration of bats. In my mind, I paired the two of them, Sasha and Ian, though now I am certain this was not only a premature pairing but an ill-advised pairing, for Sasha would grow tall, and Ian would remain short. Sasha would pursue drama and art. Ian maintained a boy's brute love of ice sports. Of all the boys I might have paired Sasha with in second grade, I understand how Ian was the worst. Any other boy might have been better with Sasha. Even an ogre named Archer, whose face appeared to have been clubbed on one side, would have been a better suitor, since virtual sources confirm that Archer has grown into an attractive and muscular adult, a turn of physicality that would have been impossible to predict. Just as it would have been impossible to predict that Sasha is currently without a lover, for she is and has always been beguiling to men and women, though more often to men. Men have always clustered around Sasha. They ask her to dance. Slip notes in her desk.

Her first college boyfriend wore heavy eyeliner and mesh tank tops. He pushed her into taxicabs, and she delighted in letting him make out with her pussy. In between, she accepted checks and large bills to accompany businessmen to meaningless dinners. She only gave head, so she wasn't a whore. Her last year of college, her boyfriend and his roommate forced their way into her body at the same time. She was pregnant only a few weeks.

I have heard that today Sasha is living in London or Cape Town, where she is trying her hand, finally, at writing. I have heard she can be found at Oxford or a private sanitarium on beautiful grounds. I cannot be sure, for I have not seen her in months, and before that, years. She attended my wedding, bringing one of her bank teller, half sisters as her date. Sasha's pupils were dilated; her hair was hennaed and angular.

A noose, gulps of pills—those whispers I'd heard.

At weddings, it's said, all eyes are on the bride. As the bride, I would like to report that this is not true. All eyes were not on me; all eyes were not on me and my new husband as we waltzed by the dais or clutched the mother-of-pearl knife handle before the cake. All eyes were on Sasha.

Sasha wore a green dress. She was still thin, that was clear to see, even at her station: seated at an unimportant table with her half sister. Sasha has always been thin, as long as I have known her. One summer, when we were fourteen, she became much, much thinner.

In a hospital bed, Sasha grew gaunt over a month, on a liquid diet prescribed for mystery stomach pains. Blood draws, X-rays, examinations, tests: Was it gout or Crohn's? Had her appendix burst? It had. Her appendicitis, I still pictured frequently, a ruby rupture in her gut. She'd left the hospital much thinner, too thin, with a scar as thick as a measuring tape from her navel to her pubis. *My scar,* she wrote me in an email RSVP to the wedding, *provokes in me no response; three men licked it, one after another, and I did not even grin.*

My new husband magnetized the dance floor encircled by his groomsmen, their ties around their heads. No one noticed my exit: I left the ballroom, walked past the pianist in the lounge, and into the women's restroom.

I saw her green dress before her face. She was staring at herself in a full-length mirror. Her waist was nothing. Champagne flowed through me: I'd never felt so earnest.

"Lovely," I said, approaching her from behind. "I'm so glad you could come. It's been too, too long."

Sasha's face crumpled then became crisp. She sounded sober: "How dare you not make me a bridesmaid? How dare you not *call* when I reached out to you? When I told you I might kill myself? What is wrong with you?"

I opened my mouth, but Sasha held up a hand. It shook, and the scar pouring down her wrist glowed.

"You're crazy," Sasha said. "I'm done with your excuses."
She was right: I had always been the fat friend.

Memo 19

Her *R*s had come from Connie C. Her *S*s, she claimed, were her own invention, half textbook, half treble clef. The uppercase *J*: hers. She worried when someone else formed letters like she did. When she was twelve, she'd tried to perfect the Neiman Marcus *N* but never quite mastered it. Her *F* was her boyfriend's, Jack's.

Today she wrote that *F* on a note to him. She'd been in his email: he wasn't just faculty advisor of the robotics club; he was screwing its president, Nomi, a sixteen-year-old with the biggest, darkest nipples Jane had ever seen.

None of it—infidelious dalliance or perfect printing—matters anymore. Her letters—stolen or rightfully, truthfully pinky-swear-on-Mother's-opalescent-bible her own, ink under her fingertips—are as helpful as the electrical tape in the console of Jack's dull silver sedan, two counties away, keeping company with a Victor badminton racket in need of a restringing. They lived in an apartment; she worked in an office. Life had become that minuscule. And stuck in the middle of

Garth Park, no letters to get her out—the Victor would only lie next to her, blades of tubular grass poking through the gappy squares—Jane stays supine while three teenagers fuck her.

#

Her mother would say this was Jane's own doing. Jane always had to skew the rules, as if a mother's cautions weren't good enough: Don't walk alone. Always bring a chaperone after eight. No dessert. Scrub your knees, those wrists.

Jane hadn't been allowed sleepovers, sports, clubs, birthday cake, or haunted houses. Wasn't permitted to trick or treat. Even in a decent neighborhood, there were crazies on every block.

Ten years ago, when Jane was fifteen, her mother had remarried. Sent Jane to boarding school. Ten years ago, her mother had called nightly. But Jane was already her own girl: Wafer-thin, wraithlike. Fucked up. When they were first dating, Jane had told Jack how she used to sit on her bed, top bunk, curled in two blankets and a sweater in the middle of Michigan—tiny art school, dead of winter—how she felt bones coming through her skin, could see ivory-soap solid after days of black grapes; heady as night darkened around her dorm and the furniture flooded with lights and colors, squares of neon on the ceiling, orange rhombuses and acid-lemon highlighter stripes slashing the chair leg where she sat and shivered from five to seven every night, listening to the phone ring during dinner.

Then spring, when Jane's face became feline, whiskered, the tendons even—she could see those, felt them in herself, as she walked through the campus woods, shutting her eyes and breathing, like her skin was nylon, paper, mesh, nothing, net, eventually transferring these mealtime excursions to scraps, stories, starts, increasingly, as her teachers—none of them lecherous, she might add—would note, "a little out of touch."

By that time, her mother didn't bother.

Later took years. A blank diploma. Her mother's divorce, another. Two hospitals. A job.

And Jane had started to begin to toy with the idea of getting better; she'd bring a lunch to Garth Park, a place she had once only seen going to and from doctors' appointments. She'd sit on a bench, bruise her spine against a tree trunk, two-hour a sandwich: she biked there with extra bread to please the ducks.

Now Jane's mother lived in another state, and Jane lived with Jack, who had no idea she would snoop in his phone (let alone his email). Garth Park was her place.

Thinking about her handwriting, about the merits of ear- or orb-shaped lowercase *A*s with the boy's thrusts, each gnash opens Jane. She's ready to split. Let her cunt tear, her lease run out. By her mother's logic, this problem is already ten years old.

#

Still. A routine Thursday. Navy partition, steel pushpins, fleshy table. Stack of tasks, Velcro cube. Was there anything worse than the office? Jane hated what her life had become: lumpy women in bunchy pants pumping sweet in coffees. Jane chewing off her lip for the taste, no water until break. Her mother had said she was gifted. Talented. And now look at her meaningless work. Gail, a hoggish biddy, hung her chin over the edge of Jane's cube and asked for diet tips because Gail's

husband liked pork, ribs, really sauce, and Jane was such a skinny Minnie. Was that her metabolism or will power, not like
Jane had to tell, but still? Still?

As of late: memomemomemomemomemomemo until
she couldn't stand the typing, got up, traded her one hour of
lunch for one hour of feeding the birds. Free. No food. To
the birds. Like a bird. Skinny as a bird. She eats. Like a bird?
Oiseau.

But anyhow, anyway, as Thursdays go, she left quietly,
passed the kitchenette hens with their upper-arm flab sleeving
their elbows, the men bill-stuffing the vending machines, stairs
by two, half ran to the metal-flaked red bike she locked outside
the small office building. She narrated herself under her breath,
old habits from obsessional days. Out. Out. Out the door, out
the building, in and—

Jane goes and leaves and comes and goes. In and out, in
and out.

8. 12. 1. 5.

The bike rack faced a holey picnic table and a pebbled ash
can, sand and sallow filters. Average. Half-smoked. She pictured Nomi's eyes, her gaze bouncing over one shoulder, that
menorah-wide ass. God, Jane was bored.

She told herself to shut up.

#

The park isn't even the sort of place Jane likes. The playground
is tedious and plastic, no teeter-totter or creaky equipment.
Splinter-proof. Round corners. Primary colors and potpourri
wood chips everywhere. Jane isn't staring at her feet and then
the water. She isn't feeding the ducks, skimming the grass,

sweating and staring at a half-dressed couple enmeshed in a brown stand of oaks.

On her back, she can blink.

The grass around her is tall, the kind to chaw. Wonderful, plenty of dirt, mud—rain a few days ago—and damp presses through her blouse. Jane is too angry to be scared.

Things: she'd wanted to see the prairie beyond the pond after all these years of being content knowing it was out there, somewhere, a blot on a map; her clothes are trashed; she'll be late to work. The boys are so big; she's so small.

One of them holds her hands, limp doves, flaccid like Jack's penis, and she envisions him, wide-stanced in front of twenty-one suburban high schoolers, teaching physics: Vs and Rs and Ps, the velocity of the member is directly proportionate to the momentum of the . . . She wonders if he'll be mad, if he'll use this as an escape. An out. But Jane went to art school. She refocuses.

The boy on top of her looks the youngest. His blue eyes, the patchy acne to the right of his nose and under his mouth, black hair curled close to his scalp. His hands knead her shoulders, the edges of her breasts, grabbing at something beyond her neck.

Jane is small. So small. Barely five feet, she weighs ninety-eight pounds. This is deal-with-it weight. Concession. Compromise for Jack. She ate breakfast for Jack. Packed sleeves of saltines. God. She has always been fine with her height. Happy. But for once, she wishes she were bigger. Heavier, taller, tougher, stronger, fatter: one-ninety-eight, two-ninety-eight, five hundred pounds, whatever would heft her out of this situation, something abdominous. To be a behemoth, massive and fleshy, to groan over and crush this boy, engulf him in skin.

She has flailed and kicked and poked and spat. Bit. She may get some disease, but at least she won't get pregnant; she's too little for that. She'll be left in this field, clothes muddied, hair threaded with limp grass—but she'll leave.

If she could, she'd scream. Scream and scream, yes, yes, oh hell, yes, scream, no, stop, and they'd leave and someone would hear her: Jack would come; she'd get help. It is so wrong—this sort of stifling. This is office-draining, clerical-dull, white walls, swivel chairs, a blacked-out monitor that glares back like a toaster.

#

She was going to feed the ducks. Locked her bike at the rack east of the pond, near the black-box barbecues and one of the two bridges, kicked off her shoes, shoes in her purse, walked, purse slung over one shoulder, stale bread bagged in plastic and secured with a twist tie, dangling from her grip.

Over the bridge and around the curves, pressing her slender bare feet into the concrete. Warm, sun-damp. Halfway around the trail before she ventured into the grass and walked to the bank of the pond.

The grass was slick and steamy. The sun blocked out the clouds. She knew it: Jack was eating now, tofu on a bun, in the cramped basement faculty lounge, using too much pepper, reading a book in silence, thinking about Nomi's midnight message: "I want to be biting your shoulder." Jane tossed a handful of cubes to the ducks. The bread floated and skittered, and the ducks dove and ruffled, sputtering, splashy. She liked their beaks' snapping, tiny plastic clamps.

"While ducks do have tongues—bumpy, muscular tongues—it's doubtful they stick them out," Jack told her, the first and only time she'd taken him to the pond. Pianist, physics teacher, nascent novelist, asshole. Sometimes he forced a finger where it didn't go. "Chinese restaurants serve duck tongue. Dim sum."

Jane had squeezed his hand and sighed. She didn't eat Chinese, and she saw ducks with their tongues out every Thursday.

#

Garth Park was named after a police officer who had retired into peanut-butter trapping squirrels in his backyard. Jane liked to imagine him, grandfatherly Garth, watching over the land. Playground, pond, picnic grove. Beyond that were the tall, feather-tipped grasses. Burr-capped reeds. Rodents with shrunken baby fingers. Native plants.

She hadn't intended to go to the prairie. She assumed she'd always be content with what she knew, the sign and the map, rules scratched behind Plexiglas, posted hours, oily ducks, watching from a distance, portioning out their small treats, what she liked: fogging up mirrors and windows.

Habits: she checked locks when she left the apartment, even after Jack was last to bed. Halfway down the hall, she would about-face and dart, checking. Coffee machine. Check. Computer. Check. Stove. Gas. Check. Outside the door, standing in the hall, gripping the doorknob, jiggling it, making sure it wasn't going to spring free, unclicking and unleashing and undoing and uneverythinging.

Jane didn't drive because of the locks. A whole house could tear her apart.

She dressed in neutrals. Seventy-five khaki and black combinations hung like ghosts in her wardrobe. Nothing dry clean. Nothing handwash. Nothing delicate. At least not in the closet.

Jane printed small. Neat. Her script looped. She showered short to save water, switched off lights in empty rooms, hibernated her computer—it reminded her of bears.

She had always liked that Jack was the opposite, that he was too ahead of himself to think of mundane things like combing his hair, which had a tendency to flip out at the bottom and on all sides and all over itself, spiraling its straight brown glory to the nape of his neck. Rancid-smelling. That he got out of bed and went.

Jack liked Jane's bureau, where black lace thongs covered a pair of unused handcuffs wrapped in a crumpled silk slip, slit up the thigh.

They worked like that.

Jack taught physics all day and wrote all night.

Jane liked this very much.

Jane typed memos all day and rubbed Jack's dick all over her face, deleted the memo, wadded up a piece of paper, shot it in the trash.

Now, though.

The whole day might be Jane thinking about what she could do at night. Typing was brainless like that, Home Row and Memo City. Jane licked her red thoughts when she typed; her brain steamed, the erratic pound of the keyboard punctuating the thrusting squeals in her head. Jane would bite her lip when she made an orthographical error, when she was dizzy, when she saw Jack's veiny hands pushing himself forward to the edge of the gray desk chair where he wrote, the way his hip bones tippled the flesh, the way he opened his legs.

Sometimes Jane caught herself typing her thoughts, writing stories from too many nights ago, a wrong word interspersed with the banalities, and she'd stop. This was an old-fashioned office. She'd pull the paper from the typewriter, fold a sharp rectangle, place it in her purse to dispose of outside the office.

#

After she fed the ducks, Jane veered off the trail, squinting at the sun hitting the tall grass, the yellows and green a static mass in the near distance.

Being honest with herself, she was afraid to live alone. Did cheating mean everything was over, start the clock, it's a matter of time, that Jack would want to move out, that she was going to have to get her own place and cook her own food and sleep her own sleep?

She'd never done it.

After a strong slope, the path emerged, a black snaking line flanked by grass on one side, brick decrepitude that must have once been a building on the other. Her mother had had a saying about unimaginative people that Jane realized she'd forgotten. The air smelled wet. Each patch of ground was two-faced, twinned, stubble and smooth coexisting she saw, so vivid, real, always changing, a contradiction she could almost touch, lifting and pressing down her feet, each step—overstimulation, maybe, due to the pressing nature of her trip, pressing in its complete and total unpressingness. She couldn't still her surroundings. Her thoughts were too fast to name.

#

Enter Ryan, Peter, and Eddy from behind an old building plopped down across the way from Jane's grassy soon-to-be bower. This is their weekend place. Their broken glass. Their knotted bandana. Their chipped Bic. Their roaches, their rubber bands, their waterlogged centerfolds, their Hostess Sno Balls.

When they speak, their tones are hushed. Watch them lurk and stare, because they're boys—of course they lurk. If there were clearer shadows, they'd be lurking in those, but, as days go, she's a sunny gal, hiding nothing, wind blowing in that fabric softener way, clotheslines and apple pies, no leftover rain buried in any of the nonexistent puffball clouds.

Ryan: That's her, that's . . . this is it, this is it. This. This is her . . . she's all alone. Look. Her.

Eddy: Yeah it is. I'm going to make that bitch suck my cock.

Eddy, shifty with greasy red hair, furiously searches the field. Even the sky is bird blank. He pushes his palm into his left thigh. He wears Levi's belted at the waist with a brown leather braid.

Peter remains quiet, nodding occasionally. He is almost preverbal. He rubs his large hands together. Warm. When Peter tries to pray, putting fingers between fingers, he turns red—his pointers are too big to fit in the spaces.

The boys were familiar with their surroundings, discrimination of the pond, vote yes for prairie fun, yes for midnight gamboling in the methed-out hobo shack, perfect backdrop, perfect town, perfect kids, perfect beer.

Perfect planning, that's what we've gotta have, mutters Eddy.

None of the boys consider Jane's breasts small, her sexual history minor league. Her skirt doesn't matter; it's only that much more convenient. When Ryan sees her walking up the blacktopped trail, it isn't important that Jane is a vegetarian.

Eddy: Shh.

(A silencing hand.)

Ryan: What the heck, eh——?

His eyes widen sans interruption, and the boys stop, pause, their pulses *pa-pum, pa-pum, pa-pum,* big, bigger, biggest, fixed stares cemented to their faces, ardor, order, guts.

#

The bag swings in her hand, dangling and untangling, twist, untwist. A few extra cubes. Crumbs. A bit of the maimed ballerina, jeté jeté jeté across the stage. Sliced-up animal caught in a cellophane balloon, toy inert in snare. Bread and bag. Air.

And that is where they pounced, clothes clinging, zooming with prurience, the pores of their pale, pimply skin suddenly swimming with sweat. . . .

From the left comes Peter, and this is where he jerks her so flippantly that she can barely comprehend these boys, their flailing eyes, poking pants, and all Jane can think about is the bread in her fist. For a minute, Jack is gone. There is *this* boy. Peter, big brother to little sister Sandy (age five), to whom he reads stories, scary ones, has only masturbated once (age eleven) and hasn't since then because he believes God will punish him (badly), but of course God won't, and neither will I because Peter is a good boy who genuflects on Sundays, likes ketchup on his mashed potato volcano, and drinks two chocolate milks at lunch. Peter weighs a hearty 250, and much of it is muscle. His swoop for Jane cuts across asphalt. Midair, Jane is petrified, stiff, and afraid to scream, desperately clutching the plastic bag, a pietà, Mary with risen leavened loaf instead of Jesus.

Ryan and Eddy dash to the middle of the prairie field, one hundred meters ahead. Track runners, both of them, during the spring. Gluttons for wind sprints. Suicides. As children, their mothers signed them up for the same high school summer running program: Up 'n Comers.

Jane speaks. Lie.

Jane cries. Lie.

Jane is hungry. Lie.

Jane likes it.

The thought enters her mind. Where does it come from? Who opened the gate? She has been good at copping her wants. She is horrified with herself, disgusted. No. This is, she thinks, life or death. No going to sleep on someone's chest afterwards, no finding just the right dip between sternum and breastbone. Jack. Violent, she tells herself. Dangerous. Fucking dangerous. She never swears. Be scared. Get afraid.

But no. Her heart is fast-beating hammer hard. Everything might change. This moment is all hers, unwatched, private, verily verily alive.

A huff and heave in his breathing, Peter puts Jane on the ground. Up close, the grass, the stems look like straws, perfect and cylindrical. Eddy yanks the bag of bread from her clench and tears it apart.

Ryan holds her hands, palms up, knuckles flat.

Eddy: She's gonna scream. I know it. Here . . . look.

Right now is when Peter, hovering above Jane, closes his eyes, still panting. He turns his head as Eddy shoves bread into her mouth, keeps shoving until there is no room for her to move her tongue, swipe her teeth, chew her gums, speak, breathe; this is going on, shoving and shoving and shoving, and no one says a thing until—

Ryan (looking her up and down): I want her first.

His voice is soft, confessional. He wouldn't be here if he didn't need this. He doesn't have to reconcile himself to his thoughts, his wants, low and molto gentle, like the throb against his thigh, dull incessancy, the blood pumping as he feels his cock extend and push against his pants, broadcloth, disagreeing with the dimensions allotted for his left leg.

Peter moves and takes over for Ryan. He pins Jane's hands. He thinks they are cold. Pointy. Sharp. Like built out of Popsicle sticks.

She watches the blue-eyed one plant a foot on either side of her. His dumb khaki crotch. Tiny wet spot. The dot of an *I*. She is wearing a knee-length black skirt, ponte, stretchy, and she curses her stupidity because pants would've been much better in many ways. Her mother always said that Jane had thick ankles. Her mother always said secrets were normal; a wife shouldn't ask, a girl shouldn't want; summer was a time to stave off your sweet tooth; no one ever really apologized. Her mother was a caustic witch.

White silk camisole, red cashmere cardigan, mother-of-pearl buttons. Nice girls: slim calves, clean wrists, ivory thoughts.

Ryan unbuttons his pants. This bitch: he notices in three seconds things Jack still hasn't seen—the birthmark above her lip, left of the philtrum; her hair, caramel intermingled with sepia and fawn. Dismissible. He wants to hammer into her until she yelps, until she breaks, until she cries, coming inside her, innermost, subaqueous commingling.

Eddy (to Ryan): Come on, man. I want to—

Ryan: You want what?

Eddy: You get her pussy. I want her face.

Peter pushes her hands into the ground, harder, her knuckles under his palms. Like there are trapdoors, rabbit holes, one more push and they both disappear. Her eyes, they're nice. His own are glazed and dull and dirty green with mites of gray, stubby lashes; he ogles her pupils like he might usually a lady's tits, perfect eyes that follow you like in a painting at a museum, behind the corneas; those pupils are so deep and round and big and black.

Jane's eyes are milk-chocolate brown. She uses mascara, $3.49, a clear tube that renders the black spiky brush visible like a miniature pine cone.

The four people in the field have this in common: they all gathered pine cones in piles when they were toddlers.

Jane hears her own breathing, much heaviness in her nose, looking down, an aberrant calm as she surveys the scene taking place around her. When will it start and will it ever stop, the fucking, these boys, the old squawk of what she should or shouldn't want, her murmury heart. She tries to slow down but everything is louder, the smell of dirt and white worms and wood and stale drizzle. A zipper, and she smells metal, tastes iron light up and down her throat. Feels the bread growing bigger, swelling her mouth, dissolving but not budging, mealing, gagging, and her skirt is hiked up, her underwear yanked down her thighs, catching at the knees, her legs she realizes are fused together, and the boy straddling her wrenches them apart, pulls the panties down, off one foot but not another, ring around the left, seamless rosette kissed anklet, and a breeze, the sort especially pleasant when caught on a bike, when her hair flounces her shoulders, and Jane thinks how nice, how nice, nice, nice, nice, thank you, whoever, for this average regular any-day breeze, mild, fine, not too warm or too cold, perfect porridge, that's what she is thinking when Ryan jams into her for the first time, hesitation a tiny mouse perched on his left shoulder.

He is too quiet, and Jane wonders if she is somehow wrong. Her body, a slop. Jack groans. His eyes lift; he talks: oh my fuck, oh my god, wow, wow, wow. Now she knows: her body isn't all he wants. He wants nine years younger. Thick curly hair. Breasts too fat to fit in a mouth. Breasts to cram together and fuck on the practice lab table in his classroom closet.

The prairie is airless, drained. Chants, cheers, boisterousness: she expects something. She wants to be someone's idea of good.

When Ryan pounds into her, he is nailing her, gripping her thighs with his down-to-the-quick fingers; he likes that her cunt is loose. That's what he thinks. His girlfriend is a tight box, can barely fit two fingers in her, and he likes that he's got time now to really get himself hot, out in the woods, wild man, he want to spill his jizz all up in her, this no-name chick he's riding. Feels so fucking cush. He starts to grunt. Moves his hands. Tears open her sweater. A button flies. Ryan twists her nipples through the blouse, watches her wince, and he inhales, shaking.

Jane can't help herself; she was the sort of child who practiced, over and over again, writing her name, signing her signature, across newspapers and shoeboxes and magazines and flesh, like she was going to be famous. Hands crawl all over, her back, like the fingers want quick recesses to fuck. Like she needs, now, she knows, to be filled over and over again, all her holes, to be the most taken, took, used.

Has she ever—fucked? Is this her first? What Jack does is so fidgety, twerky. Of course he needed someone younger. He used her for her swallow, and she could be another kind of good. Oh, restrained and filled and limited. She could spread. She could like it.

But I don't, she thinks.

I don't.

Birds, dark wingspans, beat across the sky. Partial Vs. Her dumb letters. Her stupid printing. Suddenly, she is tired of lying to herself. This, Jane thinks, this is bliss.

Rapists: the word is bitter in her gut. Jack teaches children this age, and look what he's done. He's made good. Ten years ago, Jane was one of them. Would she have done this to herself in the woods? Would she have accepted a hot breath on her neck? An inchoate invitation? Could she have dared?

Would Jack? If she asked, demanded, begged? Stop writing your book, she heard herself sass. Stop screwing that child. Taste me. Jane squeezes her eyes shut: she is alone, skirt on, sweater and buttons intact, cubicle chilly, typewriter ribbon brand new, lip waiting to be bit, hair banded back—nothing out of place.

#

Ryan is reaching some sort of climax. He fucks with more force now, rough thrusts. He imagines his come seeping through her, clouding her blood, permeating her veins, filling her lungs, every cavity for him, all his, he pumps harder and harder, and

74

doesn't notice Eddy lamely undoing—sliding it out of the two leather *U*s, unhooking the tarnished brass—his belt, taking out his penis, short and skinny, ugly, a stringy mass of blackened pubic hair, puffy and plastered down, he's rubbing one out, Eddy, he keeps on it, beating, pawing his stiff little cock with bleak urgency until the head is cherry-pink and swollen like the distended belly of one of those starving kids from Bosnia, Honduras, Rwanda, bloated on postcards at the grocery store, tummy puffed out and aching for something, that's Eddy's, one-eyed ugly slug, drops of semen clicking down, rolling off the tip, landing on Jane's forehead, he holds it over her face and wands it like a hose until she stares and stares at his dick and her eyes, close, cross, shut.

Open up, he says, and then, to himself, take it, take my come, bitch, and he jags one final time, and the stream glazes her face, eyes and nose frosted shut, and he wrings out the last of it and lets his head lull, oh god yes, bends down and smears the jizz across her face, rubbing it in her forehead and cheeks, neck nose lips. Hair.

She coughs. The smell. Batteries. Melon. Bleach. She feels her pores blocked off by a barrier of come. Coughs again. The black-haired one slaps her, and his hand sticks to her face. The come is tacky like flypaper.

Ryan's hands move back to her thighs and pinch into the flesh. He spreads her legs, further, further. His face contorts and Eddy nudges her head with his foot, watches it loll.

She thinks: This isn't enough, make it enough. More.

She wants that one with hips, a red mouth, the one holding her hand, stroking her palm, the fathead, to carry her off, sling her over his shoulder, amble home, store her in his room, feed her SweeTarts and cough syrup, let her starve under his bed. She doesn't care if he's slow.

Doll. Droll. Mall. Maul. Wall. Call—.

As Peter closes his eyes as Ryan bursts inside her as Jane tilts her neck up ever so slightly and shows off her throat.

Eddy: HA! Cunt likes it!

Oh god, yes. She does. She is wet and beating and gaped. She likes it, she wants it, loves.

He collapses on top of her, Ryan does, and Jane is still beneath his body, his heart pummeling. Eddy turns and zips up his pants. Peter rubs a Z in her right hand, just with his pinky, firm, pressing, and watches her eyes, open, barely, with the sticky, open, now they're closing.

Eddy (to Peter): Hey big guy. Your turn.

"Shut up," Peter says to the dirt. Ants. No worms. "Just shut up, Ed."

Jane begins counting in her mind. One two three boys, one two three seconds, one two three breaths, okay okay okay, on and on and on. She lies perfectly still and coughs. Swallows some bread. Again. Thick like caulk. Again, again. Twenty calories. Gone.

She is alive and swallowing, breathing, shutting her eyes. Maybe this will turn Jack on. She can see the rest of the day: The receptionist will pencil a crossword. Jane will finger-comb her hair, type eight memos, sip three sips of Diet Coke, chew and spit saltines. More memos. Timecard.

"You could have called," Jack will say when she walks into the apartment, a green pen wedged behind his ear. Jane will scratch her calf. She'll still everything between her legs. Her bike saddle. The boys. The phantom of Nomi's pendulum tits. Dinner, rufous seitan sloppy joes. Afterwards, she'll take a hot shower, scald her clit, and write in her diary, without saying good night.

But now, she's on the ground. And Ryan rises and stands, fixes his pants, the gray of dead brain. So long, Jane thinks, so long, so long. And they, all three boys, stand and survey her, their Thursday, pinned by nothing to the ground. Jane takes in the sky, the clouds and blue reversed, steamed blue against a white background, hard to know what's foreground and background, what with that mass sloping, bounding onward, and her eyes follow them, boys and clouds, the sky; it expands for minutes and hours and miles, years, compared to the office ceiling, bounded and solid. And the boys. The slick sheen covers her eyes, like the drip melting on an ice cube five minutes from the freezer.

Peter says let's go, and so they turn and walk away, from a distance visible only from the waist up because the grass is high in the field, the prairie, and it seems they were never there at all as Jane unstiffens her arms and sighs out loud, her eyes shut, holding onto the pinks and reds that mixed tangerine, great sunset streaks flaming the sky the day of eighth-grade graduation, when she sat on the roof with her best friend, sucking down her last regular soda, Dr. Pepper in a bottle with a straw.

Clambering Over Such Rocks

*P*erhaps we three shall only ever have in common the murder of Adler. And white garments, shoes, stockings, sleeves—even the body of the Pemaquid Point Lighthouse is shell colored, if you ignore her black window.

We confer at the Point, calm ourselves, and consider what we have done, firing thrice into the husband and father we have left in our Oneonta cabin.

I still see his stunned eyes stuck on a hogshead of sardines.

My mother and sister's hands smell like buckshot.

A fine spray of grayish pink stains my blouse. My father's last sputum.

Yet even now, they flaunt their them-ness, asserting their alliance against the suspiration of the Atlantic.

I cannot be blamed for growing up untouched.

#

The rocks ribbed like roof tiles. Loud water mostly mist. Sky blue as a tepid bath. One rip of sand.

Up the coast is dented. Southward, fjordlike. Islanded. Our state has beechwoods. Artists' colonies. Shore dinners. Clams. Snowshoes. Watermelon tourmaline, old Gepetto's string on silk, and fix around your neck.

#

My mother and sister stand at water's edge in matching wild berry: my mother's sweetheart sweater; my sister's maiden jumper, her billowing mutton sleeves. Flax-haired, fine-profiled victimisses.

And me, a remove from the shore, arrogating a rather smooth stone. In my Bohemian brow and trousers. A roll of flesh at my elbows.

It is my task to tip the rifle, land it in a chasm of rocks.

Get rid of the foul thing, my mother instructed me, returned to her delicacy, even after our hard travels, past OshKoshed fishermen and seals bottling, pods of whales whose rubber heads emerge like enormous bowler hats.

Once more, to the court of women's vision, I go uninvited.

#

Sometimes, my sister's skirts inflated by the crush of crashing waves, I see my mother smooth her dress, to catch it from flying up.

#

It is a tale of a family in the woods: not so special to Maine.

I, for one, have always believed it must be hard for a man to bequeath his virility to women.

What might we do, knit him a cock's cap?

Crochet a sleeve for his casting arm?

I fed my father his tinsel when he tied silver streamers.

Learned the names of artificial lures: Mud Puppy. Bass-Oreno. Royal Coachman.

I was his spread girl, the best at coating his biscuits with butter.

The best at proportioning a sandwich.

\#

It is not that I ever disbelieved my mother and sister. Poulticing their thighs would find a disciple in anyone.

And Adler's fingerprints distinguished themselves, left bruises like kidney beans.

Things he announced, daily as grace, even now aim arrows at my mind:

Your apology is but a belated excuse.

You could drive a phaeton through that piehole.

I wouldn't grope you with my rustiest fishing pole.

Only then did I realize the makeup of some women is more than a matter of pantalets.

\#

Other words organized when he took my sister to the spurrier's. When he took her out riding in a red coat. When he took her arm, held her wrist like a hatchling. She had warned me under the counterpane, how he said he wanted to spue inside her, to gild her insides like the dogwood in an ice storm.

He might have found me ready, if he'd ever come looking.

\#

The coast thinks nothing of a woman helming a rifle. She is a sportsman, clad in smaller clothing.

My legs extend in front of me. The line of my ankle is visible below the hem of my porpoise-blue trousers. It is the thin part, before muscle swells my calf.

The rifle lays long, butting my crotch. It is not much more than a broomstick. Its barrel is black and matte. It has not buckles but parts that buckle when touched.

In my mother, Adler found a wife and a wet nurse and a whimperer. When he loved her, I could hear her crying like our collie, still tender from the whelping.

A mallet, when pounding veal flat, makes a resounding bluntness. And that was the way my father's gut pummeled her rump.

#

"Bring your sulking down to the water," my sister calls, her face tear-wet and shining.

It would be salt to lick her.

It would scald to approach the limits of her love.

#

It was only once I was asked to witness.

He filled my tin cup with birch beer and set me in a kitchen chair he'd carried up the stairs to their lofted bedroom.

Midway, he flung a pillow in my lap and, grateful, I reinstated lady legs.

#

Unwelcome is not the word I feel for being a sister and daughter in this life. Unwanted is wrong, as well. More, I know I am unusable to either sex, Adler fathers, docile mothers, sisters with hot-combed hair.

(I have always wanted to ask: Do you like me?)

It is for this reason that I reposition the rifle and wedge it between my knees. Nature has engineered me with long arms, and I am relieved to finger the trigger. It feels like a latch, a hook, a malformed tack. It has known the flesh of everyone in my family. No wonder Heaven gave me such fortitude to free the shore of my disease.

The gulls overhead fight and scowl.

The black window in the lighthouse darkens.

And yes the waves roll out, folding over on themselves, thrashing at the sky. It is dim, almost aluminum. Surely, on some other horizon, there is a sun, close and gold.

Service

She wanted for certain to know she wanted nothing. None, not one. She asked herself until certainty showed, owned her—nah, she stuck to what she understood: entitled, home-tied, penned as their dog, but noisier. And hungry.

Nosier.

Time passed, but to the past the woman clung, as women are wont to cling after they have assessed themselves, trussed themselves for squandering their sixteen-ness. Weekends went. She wrote when she could, arrested Sunday pleasures, wondering would she ever be a mother. She thought away hours.

He bought her a chalkboard.

Do it! he said—less and more a husband. *Own your words!*

Church tolls rang the square. Mornings she shored at their hearth; she could not serge her scriptured self: *the fat coverth the innards . . . the offering made by fire.*

It was a morning. Had comfort massed her? Preyed on her own, that only-inside beast? She could back in or walk toward someone, something, or start kneeling alone.

This morning. Shadows cordoned the walls; the heater fuzzed. She was hungry.

She forced a walk and brought the dog.

The woman and the dog, tail perked like a plume, trotted out to the car. They lived near enough to walk to the woods—climb a hill, pass clay courts—but the dog weighed ten pounds: all that would zonk her. The dog liked scrambling up the car's back seat, hopping to the shelf above the trunk, peering out the window. Her pants smeared the glass. The woman and her husband kept a stuffed bear in the back and yam treats in the glove compartment.

The woman was happy to be alone with the dog. Her husband disciplined himself with relentless cheer. Feelings flashed off her face, and he stomached her grimaces: that irritated her, more. She was glad that he did not accompany her to the woods.

He was a man who uncorked internals and wended words; perseverance anchored his carriage. He was fit. He refused set meals, toiled, took tinctures, motored her storms. The more she voiced her frustration, the fewer her outs: she no longer polished her nails or phoned her girls.

Done with bodies, her friends wanted babies.

She passed a pram and averted her eyes. Were her friends walking, they would drop down, crouch and coo. Every infant they met, they imagined drowning with love; the woman could not. Her love was a coin she had spent in her youth. Dumb. She was thirty, nearly nowhere.

She drove up the hill and parked near the clay courts. She clipped the leash to the dog, who shot out, and soon they were inside the woods.

Sirens, bells, chimes from the distant town. On trees, leaves brizzed, slack-clasped fists; in the forest, their falling showered her.

She unleashed the dog. The dog was theirs, hers and his, one year. Daily they remarked on time, and for a year now anger yawned her face when she saw yet another cow.

She wondered if a city, larger and crummier, garbage-y, would appease her. A pal's girlfriend suffered from localized depression; the woman wondered whether she might coin her own mind's inurement.

Did she have a hurt?

Contentment?

Sure, she wondered.

Could words, hers, ever work?

First the child would wrench her apart and tear her open. She would sweat. More. Well, and clutch her stomach. Arrow splat. Her hands. Those feet. Her face. Some heart. Thick and achy ropes; her hair, she'd chew out the soap. She could bear almost anything, but lies came out of her, light and easy, layers, inches, flesh.

Coward, she comforted herself.

Cowardess!

The dog bounded through leaves. Rust and copper. The woman remembered when she had rescued the dog, maybe her one good deed. The shelter was near the college where she taught; any day she could go back on lunch. She hadn't yet, though; she would.

She would.

She would sit in the visiting room, at an uncomfortable edge on a breakable seat, envying out at guests appraising pups,

waiting. The shelter rescued small dogs, toys and teacups, an-
kle-nippers and yappies, and whole families filed staring hopes.
Old women. Piss. The place stunk—a medicinal, stewing gush.

The woman accorded the idea of a second dog, and her
husband always received it well, but she never acted, and he
never followed through, and so their one dog remained one
dog, home long days, alone.

The dog flashed across the path. She lifted a paw, cocked
her head at the frog pond. Weekends, at least the woman could
unleash the dog to the woods. The preserve. Her little girl: the
dog's eyes were lash-fringed and tear-rimmed and liquid.

#

Thoughts patterned themselves inside the woman. Maybe
the thoughts would be lost to time: others were. For instance:
when she was eight and fifteen and twenty-one and now, the
woman told herself she simply didn't want some __ (concrete noun) __
when she already held an ultimate, a pinnacle, the best. Her
baby sister was the best baby; her girlfriends, ultimate girls;
and though the woman no longer contended her baby sister
was the best baby, her girlfriends the ultimate girls, though she
believed herself wiser, she reveried the dog.

But in ten years?

She risked a crying. She could make herself sob.

That's the thing about pets, parents said, fathers.

With cheer last night, her husband had said how he would
hold the dog when something tripped. When her time comes,
he'd said, meaning time's up. When he'd spoken to the woman, he'd been smiling, calm, tears shining his eyes: he would
hold her little paw and be right there, she would know it was

okay, love would cradle her, everything would be all right, he wouldn't allow her one instant of fear, she was his woof.

Then the woman's cries: brutal, beastly. Her husband had jibed her, hey, hey, hey now, we love her every day, every day we give her the good life, hey, but the woman didn't stop.

The woman never thought of the dog's last moments, and negligence rebashed her.

Her husband out-gooded her.

#

Trails veined the woods. The dog kept along sniffing a rotted log, a wet rock, wispy withered grass. Beyond: marsh or thicket or brush. The dog loved wood chips, popcorn, espresso, flowers; the dog moseyed blocks, buried her nose in anything abloom.

Last summer, a greenhouse had assumed a vacant lot; the woman had walked the dog to the gate, picked up the dog, cradled her like a daughter, and wandered in.

A rumpled proprietress snided, as though the woman and her dog were strange. If she lived long enough, the woman would snide young women swaddling small dogs, too. But the dog's eyes, the woman saw, and her husband, if he hadn't been at work, would've found words, too, how happy, how calm their little girl looked, and the woman's heart plumped, and she sniffed the maple that nestled in the dog's fur and slow, up and down the rows, courted zinnias and petunias and marigolds and roses and asters, goldenrod, bruiseworts. Hot, mildewed, content: of a plant or fruit or body.

In her arms, the dog had panted, her pink tongue dribbling.

Dog tube. Wife snake.

The woman trailed her dog through the preserve. Bundled in a parka, her phone pocketed like a deck of cards against her ass, the woman waded in her mind, and the dog tromped. *And I will lay sinews upon you and bring up flesh, and cover you with skin, and put breath in you, and ye shall live; and ye shall know.* I will and I will, I will, she thought, but reception didn't reach the trails, and the woman recognized the pond, the planky staircase—there was nothing further.

#

Neither the woman nor her husband liked leaving the dog such long days. The high ceilings and uneven floorboards, knotty, pronounced the dog's smallness.

She's alone in her loft, they joked, but only to console themselves.

On the streets! they said of the dog, before the one about the loft.

Along the bank of the pond, the dog arched like a seal to scent scant moss; the woman watched. Romping hid the dog's teats. They washed the dog in a tub set in the bath. Almond shampoo, they would work oatmeal conditioner through her fur, and, watching a film after supper, they'd comb her with a finishing comb. Dry, her tail feathered, fluffed; wet, the woman would touch its tip and gag a little: rat. The dog's belly hair wisped in tufts; the woman would watch her husband, gentle, gently, smooth the strands over the dog's blue scar. *Does she miss her puppies?* she would ask. For years, she had been three years his junior, a fact unwilling to limber.

When the woman had brought her home from the shelter,

the dog's teats hung empty, awful sacks. Every day the woman chastised herself for almost passing over her little girl.

#

A big belluine dog approached now, unleashed and frontward from its owner, a man; he trailed. Not gruff, but rougher, rouged by hard lumbering, the man who walked on under fir cover. The woman's dog trotted over to guard her ankles.

The man was older looking, like a withered rock star, with a good gap between his teeth, and on his finger, fat bullet-colored rings. He had an expensively mussed quality, as though he had just gotten up from a plot of private dirt.

Pretty baby, the man said, covering his phone.

I'm sorry, said the woman. *She's all right.* Then, she realized the man hadn't apologized for his animal. She always apologized when unsuspecting men said something about her girl.

The dogs stood, surveying each other. Her little dog could fit under the man's dog: it was like a small cow. The woman couldn't identify the breed.

Two years old, the shelter had told the woman during the adoption; *puppies at least once, maybe twice. They shrink*—when the woman asked and asked—*but no, they couldn't be sure. She's a resource guarder,* the shelter said, explaining how a plastic hand had been stuck in the dog's food to provoke a reaction: white ringed the dog's pupils, her belly lowed a throttle. *Whale eye,* the shelter told the woman, who had imagined a yolkless white and signed the papers. This morning, when the woman poured the dog fresh water and portioned the dog's dry food, she'd lingered, dipped a finger in the water and prodded the kibble: the dog lapped and splashed her fresh water, mouthed around the woman's pointer.

The owner nodded and chummed his denier. Sunlight poured through the canopy of bare branches. The woman held out her palm, and his dog licked it.

Yes, yes, he said. *Let me call you back.*

Sweet, the woman caught herself saying.

That dog makes my day, said the man, stroking the little girl's fur.

And what is—.

Part Tibetan mastiff. All lover.

Bravely, before taking her home, the woman had strolled the dog around the parking lot of the shelter with the little girl on a borrowed, damp leash. She'd noted her jaunty step and plucky grin, her hitched hip, her revvy motor.

Now the mastiff sniffed her dog's tail, and her dog froze, eyes uncaged and tracking. There was her glottic thrum.

The woman saw syllables: dog, bird, air, sin. Her heart ticked its stun. Marriage: she could be ogled, and her mind still spun. Before their wedding, the woman admitted, yes, probably children would be prudent, yes, later; but to the doctor who prescribed her pills, she wondered how her husband couldn't know: didn't he know her? Partners, they called themselves; thirty percent of the time, the woman loved that.

Her little dog's growl curled from her throat, and the mastiff snapped.

Oh! the woman called, as her girl yapped and yapped. The woman bent and swept up the dog; she thrashed in her arms. *Lucy, NO!*

All right, enough, the man said. He bared a wide smile: two gold teeth.

I'm so sorry, she said, casting her voice wide enough for herself and her dog and her raw thoughts.

Have a good day, the man said, laughing.

She clipped the leash. Once the dog had been lost; run away from wrong done or let loose, but she had strayed and found solace, a loft, wandered to shepherd.

Shepherdess. Man and/or wife: *Thou shalt not.*

The dog panted after the mastiff and strained at her leash, leather wrapping the woman's wrist. The man, she wouldn't mind, oh he could pull her down, straddle her, make her buck as their dogs paced in watch; he could clip her, bite her, gnaw her with that hot gold mouth. Oh! Loftward. Autumn's molder slaked the woman. Shearling lined her parka, coyote at the throat.

Lamb, Goat, Tongue

*H*is landlady stopped him after she parked the van. Usually five children spilled out, but now only the woman heaved herself from the driver's seat.

She must've weighed twice as much as the man. He was trim; she was not. He fasted until dinnertime; relics of fast food littered her car. In-N-Out bags, Hardee's cups. Once he'd seen a full box of Taco Bell nachos, beef.

Breathless, the landlady greeted him with purpose. It was the first of the month; he was a good tenant, a listener.

Her smile went from curious to coy. Then she asked him, "Do you like goat?"

The man shifted his groceries. He was in the middle of making enchiladas. In a pot on the stove, cumin and oregano and cayenne tinged the oil brown. It was time for next steps. Sondra was on her way home.

"I don't know," he said.

"Well, this goat, you'll like. You'll *love*," the landlady said. Her purple eye shadow made her look young. "This is the best goat in Los Angeles. You guys want some?"

The man said, "Sure," even though Sondra said she did not eat meat. The enchiladas were vegetarian, shiitake and sweet potato, *because* she said she did not eat meat. Their fridge, however, often *did* have meat: his turkey, his chicken. Sometimes he wondered if sometimes she ate it. Goat would be no different, though he felt a little desperate accepting random meat from a van.

"This too." The landlady handed him a plastic bag, knotted at the top, with a carton inside. The inside of the bag was wet. "Goat juice."

She told him to mix it with some beans and rice and enjoy. "Let me know how Sondra likes it," the landlady said.

The man found space in the fridge, next to cashew milk and orange mostarda. As he listened to *Sketches of Spain*, his love for Sondra swelled. She said she did not eat meat, fine. She said she did not sleep well, also fine. She said she did not want children; she'd said it the other day at 6 a.m., at 6 p.m., at midnight—he put that out of mind.

He spread enchilada sauce on the bottom of a casserole pan. Outside his window, the quintuplets squealed, and then the landlady's parenting voice deepened: "NO. Get in the van."

#

Just as the enchiladas were ready, he heard heels on the asphalt. He commended his timing. Through the window by the stove, he watched the crown of Sondra's head while she climbed the stairs, the first flight.

"The apartment smells wonderful," she said.

She kept on her work clothes, which he preferred. No mention of the music. The plate he set in front of her, she complimented. He'd centered the enchiladas, sprinkled them with the salty cheese she liked, cilantro. The baby grape tomatoes had been in the oven blistering.

He asked about her day. After she told him, he spoke about the questions that could be asked of the president. They lived in a nation, they were citizens in a world beyond the two of them, and he did his civic duty, processing the news.

He was surprised she used the word *collusion*.

He lay down his knife and fork, intersecting; she, parallel. She said she didn't want more.

"Another corn tortilla won't kill you," he said, getting a second helping.

She just took garnishes.

"Did you see the lamb in the fridge?" he asked.

She licked something off her bottom lip. "I haven't been in the fridge," she said.

He sat down. "There's a box of lamb. And a container." He told her about the landlady, how this was the best lamb in Los Angeles. Then he felt angry because Sondra looked at him like *oookay*, when really there should be room for a husband to explain to his wife an abundance of strange meat in the fridge.

Perhaps because of his anger, he spent a long time meditating in the courtyard. And while meditating in the courtyard, he opened the communal grill the landlady had shown him, and there it was, a nipper of Smirnoff he kept expecting a neighbor to nick. He mined the deep well of his thoughts, and his mouth stung, worse than from the cayenne in the sauce. He recycled the bottle and returned to the apartment, where Sondra was working. He fell asleep, sitting up, on the couch.

#

Of course, marriage is composed of many mornings, and the man found the next one peaceful. It was brighter than yesterday, and he even saw a hummingbird outside their bedroom window. He meditated in the courtyard again, and this time the meditation came with clarity. He saw himself teaching a child to wrap mushrooms inside tortillas, Sondra showing the child how to use a potato peeler.

He came back to the apartment, certain this was the greatest day of his life. In the kitchen, Sondra dumped water into the Chemex.

"Goat coffee?" he said. "Pretty wife."

"Goat?"

"You didn't want goat coffee?"

She put down the water, waiting for the grounds to settle. "You said lamb."

"I said it was goat," he said.

She shook her head, smiling how she smiled when she was about to get upset. Their counselor had used the phrase *lash out.*

"Lamb."

"She said goat; I said goat. I know it's goat," he said. "I don't know what you heard."

"You said lamb," she said.

"But I didn't."

"You're wrong," she said. "But it doesn't matter."

The grounds settled. She poured them both coffee. When it was time for her to leave for work, he offered her the leftovers.

"You think if you feed me enough enchiladas, you'll make me want to get pregnant," she said. Her heels shot down the steps, toward the car.

He opened the fridge, stared at the meat, and truly couldn't recall if it was lamb or goat.

Often he had visions during meditations. Recently, he'd watched himself cutting out Sondra's tongue. In the vision, there wasn't any repercussion to the violence, neither guilt nor its wiser progeny, remorse. Just choice, decision, action, a red, solipsistic steak on the ground. No regrets. Only, in his hand, their serrated knife.

Ratchet

I

Tired of listening to the conquests of men—I slept with a black girl, a white girl, an Asian—I clung to the special horror of list-making. Time fit around me; I'd detonated the only sexual relationship I'd ever known. I could almost pass for a virgin. I looked twelve.

I lived in a city of warm Januaries and unpronounceable streets, a city of fatty ribs. I had no tongue for French. To the north, romance languages dissolved in weeds and coal. I possessed no means of transporting myself but my gut. I wanted to taste snoot.

II

The basement smelled like foot funk. I raked in fat donations until I received a title. Caller ID: 24677. I kept clean of body like everyone else. Shift after shift, I stretched foam pads over my headset. The plastic could be cleaned with some spray, a bleach wipe, but, after shift, fuzzies and ear bugs dotted the foam. So, I kept mine to my person, though it was an option to toss the plastic into a common box. But then the Yama would dump all the bags onto the counter that separates our calling center from the kitchenette, and we'd swarm, looking for the marker on our bags, the plastic sticky from too much hand grub.

The Yama, grinning, smelling like Bath & Body Works Sun-Ripened Raspberry, docking pay if you were three minutes late.

She was one woman I might become.

III

This uniformed my days. Still, my mind grazed the marrow. When I forgot my ear foams, I bought new covers for two quarters. Hopefully I had change. Otherwise, I'd say: Put it on my tab. (I owed big for a sweatshirt: IT'S NOT JUST A JOB. IT'S A CALLING!)

IV

The Yama opened a drawer of her desk and fished between file folders for her records. Oh, excuse me! Once again, my stomach mrrrrrowed.

V

Tiptoeing toward snoot, I read about tongue, one of the great cold cuts: a ribby pink baguette, quite silky. Of course, it's been in someone's mouth.

VI

The kitchenette: how many mayo packets could chill in the crisper drawer? Soy sauce packets solidify. HR women zap freezer meals. Smells slime off the film. Prick with a fork; vent with a knife.

The Yama's chunky heels clunk down the stairs. Can a big, strong body help me with the soda? Stacks of twelve packs in the back of her Camry, the green of nuked spinach.

VII

I sit next to Malcom and Eileen. They don't attend the school; they found the job online. Neither of them convinces alumni to dole out much cash, but they have their moments. Combined, they probably weigh two-thirds of a ton. Malcom is still a baby; in his eyes he looks like a shy tortoise.

I marvel at their heft, the way their bodies command more surface than the swivel chairs can afford to give.

I have a year on Eileen. She grew up a few miles from the calling center, and, two summers ago, she lost control of her Jeep and skidded across the road, falling from the vehicle, asphalt breaking her momentum on Kingshighway. Gray gravel crush and soot stripe her forearms, her elbows. She's big.

VIII

The best way to pass the time is drinking tons of coffee or water. So cold in the bathroom, I pee out my nerves, shiver off a pound.

IX

Some callers sit, near-statued, for the duration of their shifts. They highlight books; they take notes; they half-catch episodes on their laptops.

Others bob like swamp apples. Upstairs, the good water fountain. Down the hall, thermostat. Bathrooms, refrigerator, microwave, pressing reasons to run to one's car.

Everyone watches Julia, an opera singer, alabaster and apple pie, with a bodacious ass.

Taylor's family distributes fancy trail mixes, but her voice is cud, and she chews Twizzler Nibs while she talks to Prospects.

Lissa likes peanut-butter-and-bacon sandwiches, *Glee,* and girls. She's from Iowa.

Rafa wants to be Jonathan Franzen; he wolfs vegan chicken salad from recycled to-gos.

This girl Patrice, we nickname Hat—because she always wears a hat. Turns out, Hat and Eileen went to the same fat camp in La Jolla.

X

"I'm going for gastric, Jo," Eileen announces one afternoon. We hold the coveted day call positions the Yama doesn't give out to just any caller. Day calls mean no student supervisors, minimal undergrad chatter. Through the windows in the front of the room, we watch sunlight bash the bushes; the rain stutters. We paint our nails like this is the future.

Eileen is serious about surgery. She lives with her parents in a cul-de-sac next door to her grandparents. Her grandpa, Lou, built the subdivision in the 50s. Eileen can explain all the names: Louglen Circle, for instance, combines Louis, her grandfather, and Glenda, his wife.

I never doubt her mettle. Her nails are always perfect.

XI

Safest to start with the left hand.

"You're the worst at it," Eileen says, taking the polish away from me. "How come you're so smart and so bad?"

My cuticles collect spare color, my fingertips, even my cheeks. I'm very impatient: I need to suck edamame out of their pods and chew out the salt. The quicker I code my calls, the higher my Completes per hour. I want a perfect pledge.

I think: If I have a black coffee now, I'll be honey-sweet by midnight.

XII

During the day, Eileen and I seem to do nothing but remember the music of our youth. Ace of Base, we shriek. Next shift, she pulls out the CD from a piglet-pink case made of foam.

I'm speechless.

We whip through the songs so many times that the Yama emerges from her office, clenching a granola bar.

"I can't hear 'The Sign' another time," she says. Serious face.

"Maybe it's because 'All That She Wants' is hitting too close to home," I whisper after her door shuts.

XIII

First, give it a good wash. The pressed meat, bone-dry. Piccalilli on the side. I chew and feel muscle inside my mouth.

XIV

The Yama's office holds the Yama and her snacks. Quite a racket, selling—chips, candy bars, cans of pop—to hungry, high-achieving mouths. Knock on her door and watch her swivel through the glass. If she smiles, enter. If she holds up a finger, wait.

The Yama: sixty-four inches, broad-nosed, a carnivore with a weakness for chicken. Probably a B. Probably a six. She can't get enough of the vodka sauce! Don't leave her alone with the queso!

XV

Hi, Mr. Dude, my name is Joanna, and I'm a student at Washington University—how are you today? Mhmm, oh really, you're making dinner? Well, let's give you a call at another time that's better for you. No, sure, of course, it's no problem. Have a great night. Enjoy your dinner.

XVI

Things I wish to say, I can only think: *We do not eat hair, yet I give you permission to make a mouthful.*

XVII

Stick to the script, Jo, I tell myself: supervisor tone.

XVIII

I want you to go straight for my mouth.

XIX

—Yes, this is Washington University again. . . .Yes, we—.

A hang up isn't a Complete. It's an Incomplete call. Incompletes disappear into the computer. Pledges I record on a tally sheet: name, prospect number, pledge, form of payment. Some days, I'm so on fire, I burn through twenty slots.

XX

What are your talking points? Do not speak about food. Another cloudy afternoon. Another shift, on and turned on, here and there merging into a three-way call with What If—, What Will Be—, retooling the dial tone. The river reeks. I work the silence. I will not adopt a British accent. Yet I am lithe from walking in fine black shoes. My calves are trim meat. So well do I keep myself that sandwiches obviate.

XXI

I certainly hear where you're coming from. I myself am still a student and I understand that thinking about giving any little extra can be really difficult. But even a small donation helps a lot! Did you know that more than fifty percent of the money we raise each year comes from donations under a hundred dollars? No, haha, no, I'm not asking for a hundred dollars. But how about something like, five dollars? . . . Yes, well, last year you gave ten dollars. Twenty dollars? Oh, thank you so much! What credit card will that be on? A Mastercard, of course. I'm ready when you're ready.

XXII

Something very beautiful about the Yama inspires me to suc-
ceed, to do a little more than just cycle through call pools, pray-
ing no one picks up. Days in the basement, finding motivation
takes a special number. I might perish at any moment.

For starters, the Yama comes from Utah. She's half Japanese. She is the most brunette brunette. If she straightens her
hair, she looks mature; if she wets it with product, she is a teen.

We know she likes boring bands (Coldplay) and round-
toed shoes. Her business pants flare. Her nose is a crimini.
When she decides a caller isn't working out, her lips disappear, one pale length across her face. Her office door shuts. She
emerges with new efficiency, and the pop music goes.

XXIII

Of course, you still have to eat. After gastric, Eileen can only
stomach baby food and protein shakes. Once her system's stable, she brings in plastic containers no larger than a deck of
cards with halved grapes or chunks of carrot. A square of gra-
ham cracker with a thin film of peanut butter, a couple rai-
sins—she calls this Ants on a Raft.

"Jo, you're such a skinny Minnie," she says.

But later, she writes me a note on a monogrammed card:
Thanks for being a role model about food.

XXIV

No longer a role model, I miss a version of myself that could
subsist on pledges and air.

XXV

At my pinnacle I walk the park and bring white bags of greasy food. I pick at a personal focaccia for hours; I cram pasta salad into a quart and tear into packets of salt. If I'm committed, I call the Yama from a treadmill and tell her I'm running late.

"Not a problem," she says. "Thanks for letting me know."

Call, eat, call, eat, mute, chew.

XXVI

For a while I resort to PowerBars. I lay one out on a paper towel; I stare him down. My will is but a hunk of mud.

XXVII

"HAT!" barks Malcom. "HAT! HAT!" She swivels around and glares through her tinted glasses.

"What," she says, bored.

Hat equals student. Back in California, her dog Tina barks for her.

XXVIII

Once a week, Malcom's older brother, DeMarco, puts in a shift. Most days, DeMarco's an assistant at an old folks' home in Clayton; at night, he works on his record label. When the boys are together, they position their headsets askew so an earbud can stay in one ear. Add him to the mix, and the four of them, Eileen and DeMarco and Malcom, plus Hat, break the ton.

The boys teach us their hand signal: GET U SUM. We white-girl flash it until they shake their heads and smile.

Bored of day calls, Eileen and I color name cards with a GET U SUM logo. Hat is incredulous. DeMarco flips.

XXIX

See them sit in a row, four big bodies, swiveling and slurping. The boys drink AriZona Iced Tea from tall bright cans.

"I don't like vegetables," says Malcom. "Nah, nothing green." They zoom in on Nicki pics on their flip phones.

"Implants," DeMarco scoffs.

Malcom eyes the screen distrustfully. They're in Never-Givers, the worst pool, drowning. They can't get out.

XXX

Not now. Maybe later. Answering machine (Attempt 1). Answering machine (Attempt 2). Day calls. Remove from list. Do not call. Fax. Fax. Fax.

I like talking to the doctors. Most of them are in Club pools—that is, unless they only did their residency at the university, and then, the Yama reminds us, they might not feel that same affiliation, that same school connection. We have to work a lot harder to convince them.

When I sweet-talk the doctors, my voice stinks of friendliness. Fat fries on my hot charm.

XXXI

"Wanna see Tina in a hat?" says Hat.

Poor Hat. The only pictures on her phone are her and her poodle, Tina.

Monotone Hat. Tetris and thumb games Hat. Tina in a bucket hat Hat.

XXXII

Upgrade
Credit Card
<u>+ Matching Donation</u>
Perfect Pledge!!!

Where the ceiling meets the walls, the Yama tapes bright yellow stars with our names markered neat beneath a dollar amount. $500, $1000, $2500—anything big, and you're in the High Rollers Club.

XXXIII

How embarrassing: I'm the queen of older alumni: the folks who graduated before 1940. They're sweet and tangential during our time together.

One man tells me about working as a civil engineer, constructing the interstate system, how fondly he remembers unscrewing the cap of his metal canteen of coffee.

"It's a different world," I smile.

"It sure is," he says.

Upgrade: Complete.

XXXIV

The job affords me Friday nights, Saturday nights. I try dates. For instance, an adventurous eater named Hanes.

"Like the underwear. Or the wifebeaters. Whichever you prefer."

We order sweetbreads with caramel and pomegranate arils. Pig's head brightened by green apple. Tagliatelle with goat ragù.

"Jo," he says. "Great time. Next time, do let's try trotters."
He gives me a honey-bear hug and weasel grin. Smells like meat.

XXXV

"Ratchet's a ratchet," Malcom says, grinning like he's stealing
candy from under the Yama's nose. "Ratchet's texting you, cal-
lin' you."

"Ratchet?"

"RATCH-et!"

"Are you talking about those ratchets again?" (Hat's monotone.) Hat turns pages of old issues of *Entertainment Weekly*
the Yama keeps next to the glowing red Coke machine in back.
(The Yama cuts you a better deal on soda; only the HR ladies
use the slot.)

"HAT! HAT!"

"What."

XXXVI

The Yama motivates us as a group once a month. She flashes
perfect teeth. Lately, she favors empire waists. All safe colors:
cranberry, juniper, mustard. It must mean something; a pattern
is a habit born of time.

If you're the high caller, you win a fifty-dollar prize. In the
form of a gift card. To a chain restaurant or the university's
bookstore.

If we make our goals, she buys us Italian from Maggiano's
or Mexican food—taco bar!

"I love that queso," the Yama admits.

The island dividing the kitchenette from the calling center
becomes a buffet line. Plastic spoons sit in aluminum trays of

soupy beans and brick-red chicken. Diced tomato pinks next to weepy lettuce. Sour cream drizzled over the whole plate seals the deal. Chips of jalapeño interrupt the dreamy sunshine of the queso. We ladle it over plates; we make forbidden tacos. All of us get a little fatter.

XXXVII

"Do you think Brit's pregnant?" Eileen says.

The dial tones warp our brains. Daytime, we talk to lots of secretaries. We like to be nice to the office girls—we smell their aspartame breath over the phone.

Or the screech of faxes rattles our constitutions; for instance, I've forgotten momentarily that the Yama is also Brit.

"Maybe," I say. "She's been dressing funny."

XXXVIII

Loneliness is a product of talking all night and then waiting alone for a bus. Gold line, red bench. The bus stoplight flickers thanks to night bugs. What other people eat!

On the bus, I sit and negotiate my hands. They are powdery, dry from basement. I tear off a cuticle and swallow. A blind wad of soap. A coughing taste.

Once or twice, Eileen gives me a ride home. We puncture the seal of our relationship. In her car, our conversation is no longer easy, silly work chat. We gossip tentatively about the boys; we weigh Hat's moods; we swallow the real limits of the stuff between us.

"I hear Brit broke up with her boyfriend," Eileen says.

"Lissa's friends with her on Facebook," I respond. "How weird."

XXXIX

Soon, someone will see the Yama out in St. Louis. The news will wind up and down the rows of computers, amidst the burnt-flesh stink of forty processors, until no one can figure out who brought it to the calling center. What was her name? Who sat there? the student callers ask.

No call, no show.

It was me, scanning the invidious crowd, standing flamingo-legged at a heart-height bar table in Central West End; me, spending her $6.50/hr on tequila sodas; me who couldn't shake the compulsion to number my desires. Me who saw the Yama's shoulders catch the blue lights of Bar Louie. She wore a stretchy suede halter. Her martini was firefly green.

No use motiving my behaviors. I wanted to disappear and I wanted the Yama to see me: an unwed, unfed alumna drinking away future contributions to the Annual Fund.

After, I wandered down Euclid, into Straub's. Bouquet cooler, checkered tiles, greeting-card carousel; the store is closing in five minutes. Clutching a mini cart, I wobbled at the butcher counter, swaying in the salty, ferric, caloric air-conditioning, ogling the cloudy, cling-wrapped trays. The rib eyes, I remember: custard whorls of fat, waiting for me in mossy frills of parsley.

XXXX

It's only once, though, that I ride along when Eileen drives Malcom home. She offers me a ride lots of nights, but I draw lines in the sands of poverty.

I must make the most of my experiences. Alone or not, I must be a diligent recorder. I've never seen the projects.

Getting to the snoot takes us through the bad part of the city, so Malcom tells us more about ratchets.

XXXXI

By now, I can bring you where I've been. North Side, not North Shore—that's Gold Coast, another state. Here, every corner begs from a walk-up window: take it in. We're not ready for squeal.

You get a red plastic basket lined with brittle paper. Now I snoot to the curb. You sit down and graze my knee. Asphalt beneath my thin dress, your hand cups my hot thigh. Woah.

White bread sandwiching pickles and snoot. The nostrils, twin commas. Looks fine, no bristles. If I blink, the clouds in the afternoon sky spell shapes.

"Tell me what this tastes like," you say.

"Eat it yourself."

My bite is an oily whisper.

Litter

My father was bringing soup dumplings. I sat waiting on the pier, squeezing a 100 Grand wrapper in my pocket, umbrella hung on the lip of a trash barrel crabbed with graffiti. The fishermen were gone for the afternoon. They'd left sunflower seeds, creamy-shelled razor clams, the tarred spit of coffee and Skoal, the guts of their haul—roe, scales, eyelash-thin bones—betting on rain to wash away their debris.

Weather was coming. Waves leapt off the reef, tall and boastful, the ocean taunting the downpour.

I was wearing the white slicker I'd said I would. I took out the letter from my father and reread it in its entirety:

> Greetings, Earthling: We're building a landfill in Missouri. Where exactly, I'm not at liberty to disclose. You wouldn't want a landfill in your town's back pocket, would you? I'm going for broke at every meal. There's good food near the brewery, which gives away nothing about my location or the landfill's—as if they're one and the same. The brewery is ninety-three minutes

from the site. If you think I haven't thought of post-marks, think again. I was aces in Khe Sanh, after all. I'll send these dispatces from my next digs, before I begin the program.

Greetings, Earthling: With a landfill, you don't like to see movement. You don't want to. But cats and raccoons raid empty fridges. Rats couch-surf. And maggots wine and dine on anything moist. The gas is methane and basically 3D. The sound is like a neighbor popping Bubble Wrap. Last night, I ate ribs basted in Dr. Pepper, and we (the crew) played volleyball in the backyard of a bar. Fun stuff—I couldn't feel my feet.

Hey. A few days since the last installment in *Your Dad Whores Himself Out for a Dump*. This is why I trained six-minute miles, swallowed puke in pull-up drills. Ever consider how easy it is, saying shitty stuff about yourself? I blow. I have no talent. Hack. Then the good is tainted, too. The good sounds like bull: I am a superb project manager. I have a lot to offer. I control my body? Sounds as promising as Illinois Lotto. Have you ever tried spoonbread? You hardly chew it. Especially warm with maple butter.

I'm not looking forward to the program at all. I don't have a problem with my weight. You don't either, do you? Before I came "here," Traci and I had World

War . . . it was III when you were little, so where are
we now? It was your mom's deal, suggesting I enlist in
the Slim-a-thon. After she'd bought a blender. And
stopped restocking my Good & Plenty. I finally asked
why she was picking on me. We were hanging laundry in the basement, and for the better part of a load
of delicates she gave me no sign she'd heard a thing.
Finally, she got to the last bra and said I didn't have to
listen to her if I didn't want to. If my husband made a
stink about me getting sober, I'd be out, she told me,
very much her husband, snapping a clothespin. You
know she keeps Scotch in the filing cabinet down
there? I didn't.

The worst thing about this site is the air sweats. Garbage sweats. Maggots must sweat, too. It's midnight.
The sweat is huge and salty. But a worse stench lives in
my shoes. Doesn't matter that I shower. My soles are
under the sink.

This is my last morning in Missouri, Earthling. Time
to seal the envelope on this sinkhole. A landfill, if not
engineered properly, can become a sinkhole. Any surface can. You don't know when the ground beneath
your feet will open up.

I'm a week in North Dakota (expect a Bismarck post-
mark). Then I start the program. Do you ever ask
yourself if you like your life? If you fit in your skin?

I will no longer settle. For twelve weeks, I denounce garbage. I'll have daily weigh-ins with other old Vietnam boys like me. Meals like back in the mess hall. Cardio. Counseling. And check-ins. Meetings. *Other than oinking, what you been doing?* we'll say. Nothing. No, not nothing-nothing, but nothing that's settling for something. Why else eat like a hog?

Everything is possible. You weren't born yet the summer I came home. I didn't even know your mom. What did I lose—thirty pounds that June? Month, month and a half. My mother had these pans shaped like stars. If you didn't get Crisco in every corner, your banana bread stuck. A few times my mother threatened to toss those pans, but I always rescued them. She tried to rescue me, too. She was good. The way you'll want to be as a mother. She made me banana bread, greased the goddamned pans. And muffins. Or maybe I'm imagining that. Bran muffins, with stubby, floury dates.

What did I eat, you ask? Nothing. Where was I? Not in my country. When was it? No time. Or just a summer: opening the closet, saluting my uniform, and scraping breakfast into the dumb cane.

When my three months in the program are up, you won't recognize me, but I'll be in Venice on March 16, before heading to Puente Hills. I hope to see you then.

I'll bring the *xiaolongbao.*

Your fat-not-for-long father

I keep looking down the pier, this concrete exclamation point off the beach. Beyond the parking lot, the weather has emptied the boardwalk. You can't see beggars or buskers or zealots on heirloom carpets or dumpster divers hunting cans and glass. The rain has begun. It's not exactly cold, but it's supposed to last five days. I have no faith in my umbrella. It already should have blown away. Right now, I'm holding it between my knees.

I fold the letter and put it in my pocket. The rain is more than mist but lighter and denser than drizzle. The sky is the color of steelhead trout. When I look south, Marina del Rey hides in the fog. North, the Ferris wheel marks minutes in Santa Monica. I stand up, take a few steps, graze the wet metal railing with my palm.

I guess I'm searching between raindrops. Maybe my father is so thin now, I can't see him. Maybe he's already here. But there are horns on the ocean and propellers chopping the sky, and he'd flinch at those noises like me. So much like me. Nervous, jumpy, sullen, tender, not sure if this is the right thing to say.

Sound lives in the body. Sometimes I can't hear his voice.

When he comes, he'll bite a corner of the soup dumpling and squeeze just the broth into his mouth. He'll tell me that's just how you do it. Fat or skinny. Give it a try. Like a shot, he'll say. The good part, minus the bad calories. Go on. Litter, he'll say. I give you permission. He'll throw the dough into the ocean.

The Quiz and the Pledge

*T*rue and true: Wallace thought of himself as Weepy Wally, hollow-cheeked and cherry-haired. But also: the first non-binary Chi Omega pledge. A kiffle king. A nocturnal voice against the far right. Breather of *oh, Dad*. Tugger of the un-Unguentined hands of *God, Mom*, whose goodness could only be considered when their knees were next-door neighbors on the pew.

He swiped his answer across the screen, glinting in the glare. His roommate had given him a haircut, and now Wally's red was close to the scalp and feathered, and the sun was burning his neck.

He was on the patio, out back. Inside, the stovetop timer was counting down from ten-forty-two. He would hear the minutes run out. The beep would come jabby and short, like being pecked to death by a hummingbird.

True and true: He *had* completed other surveys about movies on his phone in the last three months; no one in his household worked in the marketing, entertainment, or automotive industries. He was on permanent spring break, but even back in the dorms, he suspected the twees and two-spirits with whom he shared affinities for a certain Instagram comedian and one made-to-movie graphic novel, for the cranberry wine and kimchi turnovers (he resisted), would not immediately come to mind when the app asked what comprised his household. Would he *belong* at Chi Omega? Would moving into that brick-braided gingerbread monstrosity on the sunny side of campus reorder his brain?

Wally touched his neck. It was so hot, his hand was a relief. His fingers were cooler than his palm. Even still—he got up, rotated the lawn chair, and faced the other way.

Now his face would burn.

His mother was out and thank God. In the den, his dashing dad was dunking his mustache in a midday gin and ginger. Soused sir, Wally tsked. His father liked that word—*soused.*

So did Wally: soused in the house in the south.

He tipped his chin toward the sun and watched the world darken through his glasses. Yeah, they were transition lenses; no, he didn't care. Wally leaned back, until he saw the pergola. He let melanoma souse his jaw. He licked his lips—mm, cancer. Kiffle were mostly sugar, sugar and cream cheese, sugar and poppy seeds, paddled, pulverized.

Pul—that was another sound he like. *Pulchritude, pula, Pulaski, pullus.*

He listened for the timer. When he was first back in the sunniness, Wally had spotted a baby hummingbird: *pullus.* A pulchritudinous pullus, the size of a pustule.

False and true: He enjoyed dramedies and sexy cartoons. He lived in a house where other languages were spoken. His mother trotted out the Spanish show pony. Every Uber driver got an hola.

You couldn't help what rubbed off.

It was his father's suggestion that Wally make the kiffle. And now they were in the oven. Two dozen squares, fidgety beneath the pastry wheel. Heaped with black goo. Long envelopes of calories sealed with his wet pinky.

Wally waited. His screen had stopped feeding him questions. He tapped the device, where a mandala was dialing around and around. When his mother took him to therapy, they passed a billboard for hypnotism. Had he been clouded by the sun? Something about his answer meant he hadn't qualified to complete the survey.

He closed his eyes and watched a dollar in quarters sizzle away in the heat. Laundry, a tube of sunflower seeds, a packet of Top Ramen. The surveys paid for whatever—it was Wally's call, no questions—not like his mother.

It was then the figs started falling, like a shower of uncracked walnuts. They were hard from the sun, withered after winter, and purple and green, the size of Wally's burns. His mother had tricked him, taken him to the beach shop on the pier and bought him a new Speedo—why? Just to admonish Wally.

What has my beauty boy done to his thighs! And before our Sunday picnic.

As though Wally would be serving kiffle in a kaftan.

The fig that dropped onto his phone screen was wizened, so purple it had become brown. It made a sound—Wally knew it—the plop of a fist hitting a thin thigh from up close. His thighs were tender. Bruised blue on the tops, blistered red on

119

the insides, where he'd used a cigarette lighter from his roommate's old Accord to administer the burns. No questions, his
own single in Chi Omega: was life such a miracle? Locusts,
figs, families—and birds, baby birds, hummingbirds bashing
their beaks against the hood on the stove.

Acacia

When they got off the bus in her neighborhood, she told him, "Ferrets are fur tubes with walnut brains."

It was the first time they'd hung out not in school. Even if it was just a Spanish project, they were going to her house, and her dad wouldn't be home. The ferrets would.

"I said, you down with ferrets?" She had a flat oboe voice. She wore black Converse and black jeans.

"Alright with me." He scratched his cauliflower ear. He'd given it to himself.

She started walking fast. He thought about calling, hey hold up, but his mouth was pasty, dry. The sky was the color of a faded-blue raffle ticket. It was late October, cold enough to need gloves in the morning, and in the warm afternoon he'd tied his sweatshirt around his waist. All he could do was think her name, his—he wanted to hear her use his, here, now, he wanted hers, all six letters, coming out of his mouth—but she was blearing ahead of him.

She must've realized how fast she was moving. She paused

and turned, but even then she didn't stand still. She pendulum-ed her head and her neck like an old clock. It might not have been hypnotic if he weren't high. Being high made most of life drip, slow and uneven, a pain. High, he got thinky. His doctor said he needed to stop. High was bringing him down, and he needed to be up, to like more people, including himself. He was supposed to like himself, but he wasn't sure he could. He was sure he liked her. She was weird, good-weird, even in her boring subdivision.

All around, the houses hummed aspirin-white under brown roofs. They weren't actual houses. They were townhouses. They reminded him of a PowerPoint slide, conjoined twins he'd seen in health class, a skin flap connecting two gray babies that made him put his head down on his desk. That's what townhouses in Acacia made him want to do.

He lived in Ambriance! and she lived in Acacia. No exclamation point.

"What's up, slowpoke?" she said, when he finally caught up to her.

He blinked. She was tilting her head in front of the first unique building in the subdivision. It was cabin-esque, with its own parking lot and a sign. The sign said Acacia Community Center and meant the building mattered. He was still waiting for that person, someone who made him feel he mattered. No prescription could do that, none of his pills. Not pot. Piles of dead leaves were raked all over the lawns in Acacia, differently than in Ambriance!, where teams of men hauled yard waste away in army-green trucks. Yet here the girl was, still in his day. Above the frayed black fabric of her shoe, he could see dry skin on her ankle. It wasn't rashy or scabby but sort of dusty—lightly, barely scaled, if he focused. A patch the size of a SweeTart.

He thought about, very carefully, moistening just that place on her ankle with his tongue.

"Oh crap," she said. Her head stopped tilting, and her hand flew to her mouth.

First there were rings to count on her fingers (six, gold and silver); then he traced her gaze to a house across the street. A squad car hugged the curb, lights strobing, no sirens. He saw two police officers pinning a man in a red flannel to the yard. The man flailed in the leaves, sending leaves everywhere, thrashing against the officers, kicking up at them.

"I don't do drugs, but if I did it'd be heroin," she said. "*Not* meth. Not bath salts."

"Do you know that guy?" He pointed to the man being held down.

"Yeah. Yes, I do," she said.

She suggested they take their studying to the gazebo in the park.

#

They went to a field behind Acacia Community Center. Dry grass crunched under their shoes. It was so quiet. Fall is the quietest season, he thought. He took a pen out of his pocket and wrote that on his arm. He couldn't tell if she was upset. He wanted to say the right thing.

"You're excited for the Spanish Civil War," he said. "Been there."

"Juventud, divino tesoro."

He tried to think of another one of Senora Llañez's proverbs, but that was the one he had remembered, too. The poet Rubén Darío.

He hurried with her now. He sensed a change, like he'd joined a mission, a brigade. They passed tennis courts locked behind chain-link fences lined with forest-green mesh. He wondered if anyone was watching them. His (almost ex-) girlfriend loved chain link.

"It's nice to have tennis courts close by," he said. "Do you play?"

"They're clay. I guess that's special."

"I don't know if you're being sarcastic," he said.

She smirked. "Okay."

The gazebo was right there. It smelled of new lumber, but the wood was ashen, like it had absorbed many thunderstorms. The girl went to a metal switch plate next to the doorway, and the inside lit up.

It was kind of lame, this gazebo. There was a bulb in a wire cage mounted from the ceiling. One long bench wrapped around the interior perimeter. There was a picnic table in the center and a steel-drum garbage can stenciled PROP. OF ACACIA and a floor drain. He thought about all the people who had peed down that drain. Probably lots in this area.

The girl set her backpack on the table and stood a minute, rubbing her skull. She took out her ponytail and looked relieved. She had a high forehead, and her hair down balanced that out. But to him she was pretty either way. He liked how in one of her eyes, on the sclera, there was a permanent dot of blood.

"I didn't think he'd be so frigging dumb," she said, abruptly. "To try that."

He put his backpack on the table next to hers.

"Your dad?"

"No, Federico García Lorca. Getting himself murdered in Granada."

"Stupid fascists," he said.

"Stupid dads."

He took out a binder. He couldn't get settled (legs, always in the way). He crouched on the bench seat, looking at her shoes.

"Okay, what do we need to do?" she said.

He flipped to the green tab, which was Spanish. She was still standing, running her fingers through her hair, combing out snarls. He could hear each pull.

The first page in this section was the assignment sheet. It had Xerox vomit and clip art of a frigate beside the flag of Spain. There were vague instructions:

1) **Define** context of historical event.

2) **Explain** inciting incident.

3) **Provide** human testimonies, examples of relevant art, and other reactions.

4) **Explore** consequences and influences on Spanish culture today.

He pushed the binder into the center of the table like a declaration.

"One thing we can use is this vow from these nuns." She took out a book called *Blood of Spain* and read from it:

The Margaritas of Tafalla solemnly promise on the Sacred Heart of Jesus

1. To observe modesty in dress: long sleeves, high necks, skirts to the ankle, blouses full at the chest.

2. To read no novels, newspapers or magazines, to go to no cinema or theatre, without ecclesiastical license.

"It goes on," she said. "No makeup while the war lasts, yay Jesus. Yay Spain."

"You think that counts as testimony?" he said.

"Sure," she said. "I guess every reaction is kind of testifying. To something."

A dark look crossed her face. She climbed onto the picnic table and tented her legs, hugging her knees. He saw smears on her jeans, a pasty greasiness on the black, like what a dog left after it had licked glass.

"What's up?" he said.

She tilted her head, only once. "Do you know anything about horny toads?"

"Is that a sex joke? Horny toad?"

She shook her head, with that same dark expression. He joined her on top of the table. *(Do not be alone in your fear* his doctor liked to say.) It was hard to look at her and also hard not to look at her, so he tried to glance on her face, the black makeup smears on the bridge of her nose.

"Horny toads are actually lizards. The name is a misnomer. But what they are is really freaking ugly. Like mini dinosaurs. There are lots of them in Texas."

"You're not from Texas, are you?"

"Y'all have to wait and see, huh? . . . No. But my asshole dad is. Eastland."

Outside, the sky was a bruise, a bluing gray that heightened the color of the trees. They were maples, still holding copper in their leaves, scattered about the field, each staked by itself in the middle of a mound of mulch.

"He had to take over after my mom couldn't handle me," she said. "There was one horny toad who lived for thirty years in a courthouse. In the cornerstone of a courthouse."

He nodded. He wondered what she would look like in a velvet dress, a particular grungy velvet dress he had seen on a singer on MTV. He had never seen the girl in a dress. He had known her since August, when he sat next to her in the front row in Spanish. He liked to be where Señora Llañez could see him. He liked to be called on. He was good at the language because he talked to the landscapers and brought them Diet Rite, also the housekeeper before Dawn, Irma. It had been last month, on a field trip to Emilio's for tapas, where they tasted the potato salad (mucho ajo) and drank virgin sangria (when his girlfriend announced he was too motherfucking loco for her to speak to him in public), that he watched this girl be a class act.

"And then it died?" he said. "The toad in the courthouse?"

"La lengua no tiene hueso, pero corta lo más grueso. Or, I guess, the thickest lizard."

"I have no idea what you're talking about," he said.

"Words can hurt. To put it lamely."

He watched a worker with a bandana under his baseball cap approach one of the maples. The man had a plastic tank strapped on his back that connected to a hose in his hands. Angling the hose at branches, he started blowing down dead leaves. The noise was muffled, but the smell was loud hot fuel. The leaves came down in sharp grabs.

He looked back at the girl. "I know what you said, but I don't know what you mean. What do you mean, *couldn't handle you?*"

The girl's knees butterflied open. Every year since sixth grade, a kid claimed he could fellate himself in this position: at least he'd never been *that* sick.

"Do you mind if I take off my shoes?" she said.

He shivered at the thought of her feet. Maybe he would become a man who masturbated on toes, some desperate decade in the future. He didn't rule anything out. He might own a boat, become a lawyer, get ticketed for jaywalking across LaGrange Road, lose his virginity to a transsexual man, swallow a bee on a cupcake and get stung in the esophagus and die without leaving the country. He'd begun stockpiling his meds. There were so many ways to be somebody, and life always put them out of reach, in the distance. The light in the gazebo was waning. The worker was gone, the tree denuded. A siren wailed. They both turned, even though the street was out of sight. The girl untied her shoes. She was wearing low-cut black socks that curved just below her ankle. She started to scratch the dry skin.

"I was getting these headaches. I thought they were migraines, without any of the auras. You know what those are?"

"Mom gets migraines," he said.

"You're one of those people," the girl said. "Mom. Is it *Mom*? Does *Mom* get migraines?"

"Mom does."

The girl smiled. "Okay, so I was very disappointed. Because if I was going to have headaches, I wanted to have the full experience of being . . . I don't know, altered. It's like the closest I could come to being high."

He picked at his jeans.

"They were so bad, I would have to lie down if I drank a glass of milk or if my mom had the TV going or when she was having a cigarette—especially then. Finally, they were so bad I couldn't read. I'd open a book and watch the letters just swim."

"Jesus," he said.

The gazebo did not provide much barrier from the wind. "Anyhow, this culminates like every good story in a trip to the El Paso ER. Which, let me tell you, is two-thirds nacho-eating and one-third pistol holsters. So that sounds funny, but I'm scared. I think I'm going to . . . I start telling myself that I have a short lifeline, that I'm destined to die at fifteen, that this is the trajectory of my life, and I'm terrified. I don't want to cease to exist in the El Paso Emergency Room. I don't want to stop smelling nachos. I'm there, with my mom, who has had it up to here with my headaches. And finally they do X-rays. I had to get an MRI. And I'm in the tube for about thirty seconds, staring at the ceiling, where they wallpaper it with a sky to make you relax—"

"That's pretty uninspired," he said.

"So just listen," she said, shortly. "The lights flash on and off. The grinding thing that happens with an MRI just stops. And I think, maybe I am dead. That when you die, it's just that." She snapped. "Quick. And maybe you don't know. Maybe you'll just keep going along . . . thinking. . . ."

He didn't want to say anything. Her finger was working exclusive of the rest of her body, digging at her ankle in surprisingly even gouges. He saw a 3D chunk of skin fall off and, without thinking, he grabbed her wrist.

"Please stop," he said.

She yanked away her arm but fisted her hand in her lap.

"What's in my head is a hundred percent unique," she said. "Not one other person alive today can claim to have a horny toad in her skull. The end."

He coughed on a laugh. "Fuck you, horny toad. No way."

She raised an eyebrow.

"No way," he said again.

"There's a lot about me you wouldn't know," she said, quietly pleased.

He didn't want this, but he felt himself starting to like her less. He fit her, quickly and immediately, into a mold. She was a quirky girl, a girl who loved cats and black nail polish and tarot decks and occult legends. Fine. She was a girl who carved Wiccan symbols into her thighs and filled in the grooves with a Sharpie. Okay. But she was also a weirdo who made up implausible things to catch you in a game of gullibility (sick-making, that same sad-queasy sick, Siamese twins and townhomes and warts), and he was so tired of being tricked by people who pretended to have a personal interest in you. *Dear lord*, his mother used to say when he started crying, *would you just be quiet.*

The girl picked up his hand and read what he'd written on his arm.

"Why do you think this is the quietest season?" she said.

He gave her a blank look.

"You seem like you have something you want to say to me," she said. "You still can, you know. Even if I do have a horny toad. His name, by the way, is Duke."

He shrugged. "What did you say? I was thinking about this stupid poem for my girlfriend," he said, "and I got distracted."

"That's everything?" the girl asked, flinching.

He stared at her ankle. Otherwise, all he was thinking about was Spanish.

#

They took notes until it got dark. The girl got up, switched on a second light in the gazebo, and they worked more. It got

colder, and the wind didn't stop, and he was hungry and thinking about what Dawn would make for dinner—he was having
a hard time focusing. Eat, drink, sleep. Sex? Sometimes, his
girlfriend would let him do what she called tapas sex. It was a
joke she'd come up with after they learned, last year, how tapas
were invented in bars in Barcelona, with glasses covered by saucers to protect the drinks from bugs. The bartenders would put
food on the saucers. His girlfriend said he could consider her
his saucer. Basically, tapas sex meant he masturbated and came
on some part of her, usually her forehead.

"I should probably get home," the girl said. "The ferrets
need to feed."

Walking back through the field, she was in front of him
again. He thought about how, just a couple hours ago, he
should've pushed the girl up against the fenced-in tennis courts.
He regretted that. It seemed to him that if he had kissed her,
if he had pressed himself into her, she wouldn't have invented
a frog in her brain to—what? Codedly explain her dad was a
junkie? Hint that she was depressed? He didn't understand.

They walked up the driveway of the house with the lawn
where the man in red flannel had been kicking leaves. The girl
tested the knob of the front door like it would be hot. He saw
her shoulders relax as she used a key hooked to a jungle-green
rabbit's foot.

"Do you want to see the ferrets?" she said, flipping on the
hall light.

He peeked in. The townhouse smelled like piss and garlic sauce. There was a dartboard in the hallway and a bunch
of foam darts on the floor, which was carpet, a camouflage of
stains and burns.

"I would love to see the ferrets," he said.

He followed her down the hallway. There were doors on both sides, but they were all closed, and it was longer than he'd expected—it felt more like a crummy office than a home. At the end, they came to a door with a poster of John Wayne.

"The Duke," the girl said. She smiled. "It might smell."

She opened the door. He wanted to turn around, but he could only go forward.

He had expected the ferrets to be in glass tanks; they were loose. Running, moving, wriggling between a small white desk and a canopy bed, they shrieked *creeee* (a shrill like two-dozen ibuprofen in your stomach), and there were four: one mink brown, another sable, two others white.

The girl made kissing noises. Her face brightened; her eyes were gleaming. She knelt down, and he stared. He felt a little sick. He was jealous. She looked so happy. The ferrets dodged his feet and swarmed her ankles. The minky one ran up her arm and clutched her neck with its paws.

"The most remarkable thing about the horny toad is its venom vision," the girl said, only half to him. "It can shoot blood out of its eyes at its enemies. That and the fact that, with me, it's in a symbiotic relationship. My toad must be the first toad to live in a human, and I know I'm the first human to live with a toad. A toad at the brain stem."

She rolled up the cuffs of her jeans.

"Ferrets, on the other hand, need meat." She stroked the tiny head of one of the white animals. There was a rust-colored stain on its little capped skull. It had a pink nose; it was a snake, a mouse, and a cat combined. "These guys should eat ten times a day. That's why I let them sleep with me. I'm an easy nibble."

She pointed at them, one at a time, when he asked if they had names.

"A, B, C, and D. My dad's such a fuck-wad that he didn't give them names. A is Anorexia, B is Bulimia, C is Cutting, D is Depression. Some girls get problems. I get pecks. Love pecks."

He watched the sable ferret sink its tiny triangular teeth into her index finger. The back of his neck was itchy. He said he probably needed to call his ride.

"In the kitchen," the girl said, over her shoulder. "It's a red rotary on the wall."

#

He hadn't used a phone like that in years. His girlfriend didn't answer, obviously: she had called him a crazy, out-of-touch, elitist, stoner maniac. He stood on the porch, wondering if the housekeeper, Dawn, would smell ferret piss on him when she picked him up, and was surprised when a station wagon turned into the driveway. The man in red flannel got out.

"Evening," the man called. He sniffed. "You're a little late to rake leaves."

"Pardon?"

"I said, it's about dinnertime. For me, anyhow."

He stepped down from the porch. He didn't mean to take a deep breath, but that's how it happened. He was thinking, *be cool, be very cool. This is the father of a girl who matters.*

"I was just working on a project with Portia," he said to Portia's father. "Spanish."

The start of a gibbous moon was stuck in the sky. There was an owl.

The man looked at him. "Portia."

"Portia," he said.

"She hasn't really been up for much company since the move." The man pulled a hair ball from the nap of his flannel and dropped it in the yard. "I'm surprised she didn't ask you to do the leaves."

He shrugged. He hoisted his backpack and started walking down the driveway.

#

Acacia didn't look any better in the dark. Actually, it was worse. Now the homes had hollow blue TV light filling the windows. He knew Dawn would see him on the street, and she would sense that his mood was plunging, and that made him feel guilty on top of feeling awful. This was the way so many people spent their lives: fit into identical houses, pointing their faces towards sitcoms and sports. He smelled something like hot lunch tacos. Then he heard sneakers slapping.

"Ethan!"

He turned around and stopped. Portia was running. When she got close, he could see her shoelaces weren't even tied.

"I forgot to tell you," she gasped. "Turkey parachutes. In the Spanish Civil War."

He looked at her. "What?"

She took a breath. "Okay, so another thing about nuns. It's 1936. There's a monastery in the mountains that needs stuff. Delicate supplies. So the Nationals make bundles and attach them to turkeys . . . live turkeys. And then they push the turkeys out of planes so the supplies land safe and the nuns can survive . . . on turkey meat. Which sounds cruel, but . . . even though they were basically isolated, they survived."

When she stopped, he told himself to do it, and he did: he bent down and kissed her until their mouths tasted like blood.

She stared at him. He wanted to say something else, but he couldn't get himself to, so he knelt down and tied her shoes.

#

On the way home, Dawn made a show of plugging her nose. She didn't speak Spanish, but he said it anyway, *juventud, divino tesoro.* The gatehouse attendant waved them through. He had time to scrub up, Dawn said. They were having quiche and green salad for dinner, and Mom was working late. (Fine.)

Alone in his room, he ate the last of his marijuana gummy worms and let his mind unfold. He shook out his stash of pills on a study abroad flyer and moved them around like tiny checkers pieces into a diamond, a circle, a spiral. He even took out a piece of loose-leaf and a pen, but he could only think of the Spanish word for frog. "Rana." He put the paper away. He sat in his underwear and turned on his computer and started reading about *Phrynosoma.* Horned lizard. Horny toad. It was pastel-scaled, he read, its coloration "pleasing" and "sandy." One image showed it beside a teacup, and it really was small. Another put it next to a cigar called a claro. He scrolled and clicked and felt a sadness he couldn't put into words. The sturdy creature, he learned, was becoming rarer. A few scientists blamed a siege of fire ants, but mostly the consensus was deforestation. There was no way for an animal to survive without its habitat.

Rio Grande, Wisconsin

The Egg is a prison. The air-conditioning is stuffy and sweet, thick and cold. When you were younger, the windows in the back seat of the station wagon opened in one direction. But in the way back, you're twelve, and the mechanisms have changed. You're getting too old for family. You're not meant for Hi-C, Shark Bites, pretzel rods, snacks. You are a void. You want to swallow everything: cheese spread, plastic straws, chocolate milk Chugs, the draggy strings off towels.

#

Menace. You've been called this by your mother and your father, your swim coaches: adults you're stuck with. You have menaced swimmers with grabby hands. You have menaced your house by staying up all night, by flashing Shilpan Patel across the street. You have menaced your mother by being bigger than her. And now you menace the Egg by being yourself, bare feet pressing against the passenger window. You know what you want: you want to push your toe prints through the glass, shatter the window, and shred your ankles.

"Wanna play mercy?" you ask your brother, Lawrence. His menaces are different than yours: little-boy blunders. Canted smiles and loose teeth. He has flushed a frog down the toilet. (You suggested he was a serial killer in training, which upped your menace.) One more log for your mother's bonfire, the one that'll be doused by the child psychologist she's found for you.

Lawrence leans over the seat. You bend his fingers backward, until his bones crack like Legos.

"Give in!"

"Yes yes yes—ow!"

"Francesca! Stop tormenting! Don't be—"

Behind her softball-sized sunglasses, your mom's eyes are slits, but you see her disgust: the mirror image of you.

"Why do *you* torment *me*?" Sometimes you imagine you are wearing a plastic space suit to protect yourself against her vitriol, but this vacation, you're getting naked.

"Don't back talk your mother, Frankie," says your dad. He sits spread-legged, Rand McNally's Midwest mapped across his lap. "Leave your brother alone. You're bigger than all this. If it happens again, it's on the list."

Squeeze your eyes shut and pretend to sleep. Dreams taste like the watermelon Jolly Ranchers you get during speech team after school, where you're friends with witty drama boys, not stuck in swimming pools or locker rooms, not always wrong.

At school, there's no list.

\#

The Egg steamrolls the mysteries of Illinois. Congestion clouds the rickety Spirograph of American Eagle, the one wooden roller coaster at Six Flags. The world is smokestacks and malls and outlets, Amoco and Woodfield and Gurnee Mills, hick towns like Rockford and Rockton, Belvidere—home to a Chrysler plant your dad annually points out. He harbors hopes: his daughter might be an athlete (you're a grass twirler). An altar server (you get laugh attacks during homilies). A mathematician, except when he tried to teach you multiplication with As and Xs, you said, "Math, not language arts." He set down his graphite pencil, the eraser-less kind for geniuses. You were a disappointment.

You try to sleep in the Egg, but you are not an easy sleeper, not with the Patels' lights across the street, not with *Private Lives* on the radio, not when you're trying. Trying, you're almost guaranteed to fail. You meet your body: left eyebrow itch, right eyebrow itch, third eye itch, lower left chin itch. You feel woolly. How long since your parents took away your tweezers? You've been forlorn.

Peek at the world out the window, Loves Grove's picnic benches and steel garbage drums. You know the town by its water tower: red bubble letters trapping a heart, the silo dirty-sock white.

#

Welcome to Wisconsin.

Interstate signs announce Beloit. At a college there, your dad's brother, Pete, smoked away one semester, selling term papers and dime bags out of his sarsaparilla-colored Cadillac. Then Janesville, where the Harley dealership outfitted the entire Novic quartet with screaming eagle T-shirts (yours too tight across the boobs) and you ate your only Wendy's meal (a kid's Frosty and a square cheeseburger).

Your eyeballs burn salty. Your parents think you are asleep. Your parents took your headphones, too—you were "obsessed," your mom claimed. With what? Third Eye Blind? Stephan Jenkins's words, singed on your brain?

You wish *you* could "cut ties"—lies or no lies—at least with your family.

Instead, you hear your parents.

"Leave these two in the room and hit the beach? They're old enough. Let's get wild."

"Diane. Nasty mouth. You got a taste for summer? You want me to hide you in the lake? You want me to give you something to drown in?"

"Tell them we're at Loots. That'll scare them."

Two hours from now on River Road, the last turn before the Hotel Rio Grande, your family will drive past the wooden sign for Loots: forest-green writing on an ivory background, the painterly woodpecker—not a nature preserve or a camping ground but a supper club. *Are you ready?* your dad will say. *Let's make it good,* your mom will shout. *Loots salute!* Then, in unison, you four will stick out your tongues. *BOOOO!* You will feel tricked into wholesomeness, togetherness. You will want it. To believe your family is a team.

Loots is gross. You don't remember the meal or how old you were, just the aftermath: your mom and dad barfing, your brother crying in the hotel bathroom, sick from both ends. You've never puked, but still. Bodily expulsion: that's your Novic thing.

"You know I get hungry in the sticks." Your mom's giggles are slutty and delightful, something you shouldn't hear that gives you hope that someday, you, too, might tread lightly enough in the world to giggle with a man. You peek at her: she's hair. Hair over the seatback like a blond pastry, glazed and pear-scented, a curlicuing snail. She's a fox.

In the middle seat, Lawrence is missing this. He spazzes his Game Boy. Life-preserver headphones bear-hug his skull. You catch weak burps of the Mario theme, the dribble of notes that means Yoshi's tumbled down a hole.

Your mom's glance lights on your dad's lap, where the map bunches everything north of Wisconsin. They've been in love since college; they used to camp. They have had children, terriers, houses, cars, a mirror over their bed, a Jacuzzi in their bathroom. Once, you had a friend. Michelle. She came over, and you showed her your parents' room: the adobe pillars, the fern-green shams. Then your mom walked in when Michelle was telling you how she'd spread peanut butter on her hoo-ha and her dog had licked it off, professing that she, Michelle Zandra Harmon, age ten, loved oral sex. That was the end of friends.

"You'll be my sugar?" says your mom. "Like the days you used to dance?"

"Di, you know I'll make it good for you, honey. Big and good."

Swallow a retch. Two years ago, mistaking this stripper malarkey for truth, you boasted to the swim team about your father being a pediatrician *and* an exotic dancer. When this rumor got back to your mom, she asked you, "Seriously, honey, who made you so dumb?"

\#

Exit 13. Cheese Haus, Swiss Maid Fudge, Stein's Garden, Cave of Wonders.

Between your thighs, you ride an awkward bump of denim shorts and stifled rage. Under your T-shirt, your sports bra is white cotton, the elastic peeking through a flesh-colored frown. Tired of listening to your parents' dirty talk, you have been trying to think yourself off.

Goo in your underpants. You need to blot the wet.

Mental masturbation is a secret your parents haven't discovered. The fantasies are you and Bill Murray—in your head you call him Dr. Bob. Dr. Bob is hunky, and his specialty is 100 percent Frankie, her eyelash flutters and nose squinches and extra cake-batter lip gloss. He doesn't need a Clearasil blast like seventh grader Aaron MacMahon, your class's most popular kid, whose skin is ground beef. Dr. Bob sees you. He's there for you. He uses you.

The Cheese Haus looks like a chalet, a Bavarian appendage of the gas station. You love things that are versions of something else. Replicas. When you were little, you had a set of Russian nesting dolls that you lined up. It was the largest woman that fascinated you. Her big lips, her almond eyes: she housed all the others.

"Let's get fudge! Or cheese curds?" you ask. You try to remember your place—heading to the Dells with your family. Sitting in a minivan—not Dr. Bob's dingy, cramped, carpeted, crusty-with-instant-coffee office, which smells like caramel and bread, like hiding under an afghan in the center of a rainstorm.

"Frankie, it's a vacation, not a binge," says your mom. "You know you don't want that garbage. Really. We're just getting gas."

This sexy body won sixth place in Conference? Dr. Bob says. *Fly? You little slut. Lots of hip action with butterfly.* He lifts your heavy black ponytail and slings it over your shoulder, princess-style. Beneath your butt, his magic penis transforms into a wand.

Your dad swivels. His minky eyebrows leap over his sunglasses.

"You know that magic ratio of fat to protein? Oh no: we don't need Lare-Meister to get his own special gas. Larry Lactose!"

You groan. You too had cutesy nicknames. Frankie-Spanky. Why? You spanked your stuffed animals.

Your brother wears a shirt printed with stegosauruses and a rainbow bucket hat. He can eat sorbet, goat cheese, and soy milk.

You unbuckle. Between your legs is sick-slick, near success.

"Can I go to the bathroom?"

"Di," says your dad. "Frankie's hitting the pot."

#

The pot is unisex: your bacteria are no different than Dr. Bob's. You hover over the toilet. Your hamstrings quiver. With a wad of toilet paper, you wipe the albumen glop from your crotch.

With your shorts unzipped, you waddle to the sink. On a poster, androgynous hands crawl with amiable germs. In the mirror, you are block shaped, wide without curves, despite the Levi's tag. On the wall behind you, a dispenser sells pads and Rib-Her-Up condoms.

You lean against the sink. Make a fuck-me face, stop your thoughts, be blank. This is what it would be like to be desirable. Sexy.

You have this hobby: you think all the bad thoughts in your mind to prove that you're tough. You don't know why you need this, but you are sure, very sure: you need to be brash. Abrasive. Vile—if it's Mother talking. "Facedown on the mattress," sings Stephan Jenkins. *Swoon.* You do it now: oh, you love your stomach, *cummy tum tum.* The skin around your navel, sticky-warm honeycomb. Cummy-comb. You touch your mound, where the hairs you plucked are already poking back. Nice cum bucket. The first item on your parents' list is *naked at pool.* You would show yourself to anyone. You cock your head at your reflection.

#

When the Egg stops again, you're at Hotel Rio Grande.

Hola, Wisconsin! In the parking lot, across from the hotel's outdoor waterpark, taste the cardboard fuzz of waking up. Your last week at swim practice springs to mind: before Hillary the mannish coach called your parents and told them you were the only thirteen-and-under girl—actually, the only girl—showering "au naturel." And another complaint: the phone call from Mrs. Dickinson, delicate Claire's mother, Claire who has a blue vein waltzing across her forehead and toenails so long they remind you of piano keys.

"You disturbed a sensitive girl with your exhibitionism"—that's what your mom told you.

"We're here, here, here!" yells Lawrence. He flips into the way back. He lands on you, and you feel how small he is. Your body is sluggish, a lumpy tube. "Frankie, you missed Loots salute."

"Why didn't you guys wake me up?"

"We've done it lots of times. Big dealio. You wanna see Lake Delton too?"

You roll your eyes. Your parents no longer camp near or fish or swim in open bodies of water. If you swam naked, your vagina might swallow a minnow.

Many buildings comprise the hotel, pink and adobe style, with cinnamon terra-cotta roofs. Behind a red fence, the water park is Southwest on steroids: An upside-down sombrero rains Listerine-blue water, and a sea of saguaro cacti shoot Super Soaker streams into the cloudless, shimmery Wisconsin sky. You are excited—for tube slides, dunk station, wave pool, secret nachos—until you remember the list. The stack of grievances, a report card your parents are keeping: enough bad grades, and you'll be barred from adulthood.

"That's all new this year," your mom says. From palm tree-disguised loudspeakers comes a double-time techno remix of "La Bamba." "There's a fitness center, sunrise yoga on the pavilion. That's what I'm psyched for. Vinyasa in the Dells? Gila Monster's Juice Bar? Delicious. That's for Frankie and me."

"Frankie and I," you say.

"No, sweetheart." Her voice is taut. She's so pretty, you forget she's smart. "You're wrong. We're the object: Frankie and *me*."

While your parents check in, Lawrence and you browse. Once you wind through the Mesa Grille and Pueblo's Lounge (you steal a handful of Gardetto's snack mix, drop everything but the rye chips on the dark carpet), you're at reception and Rio's Grand Bazaar, a glassed-in room smaller than your closet.

"*Don't* break anything," you say. Klutz is your nickname. You're compensating; you know—you love to reflect on your behavior. That shrink will eat up your brain.

But Lawrence is hiding inside a rack of T-shirts printed with smirking Mexican Fire Barrels from the Dancing Cactus show. You hear him inside the hangers.

You pretend to examine a purple mesh cover-up with dangling strings and red, green, and yellow beads. More holes than fabric. The merchandise is so trashy. Cheap. Why do your parents keep coming back to this hotel?

"*Don't be a cooz*," your brother says. He smacks you on the back.

You wince, more than the slap warrants. *You like drama, Spanky,* whispers Dr. Bob.

"What did you call me?"

"A snooze." He shakes a snow globe in your face, shimmying his rump, while glittery flecks of bronze sun rain over a miniature Rio Grande.

#

Room 705 smells like hair dryer and powdery floral spray to deodorize the last people. There are versions of Novics everywhere, a little nicer, a little meaner. Some of those other yous slept in this room, where the wallpaper zigzags like bleached Tetris.

Your mom whisks off bedspreads and throw pillows from the beds—they look naked and small in their plain white sheets, without their Native American covers.

At the window, you finger the metal-balled chain for the blinds. The view is so private, more hidden than your bedroom window, where Shilpan Patel flashes his camping lantern for a peep show. Here, the swath of evergreens is a patchy quilt sewn with argent gaps of river. It's pretty, and there's no one watching.

Your dad opens the bathroom, tests the fan. He straddles the doorway between abode and commode and clears his throat.

"A man needs to christen his domain."

"I'm unpacking, Jer. Run the tap."

"Can you send them—?"

"I'll get my suit!" yells Lawrence.

"No," your mom says. "Frankie. Get ice. Bring him, okay? And really—stairs?"

#

You and Lawrence pass through the hallway barefoot. The wallpaper is corrugated; it makes a snaggy zip under your finger. You touch everything. Your brother runs, leapfrogging the carpet, pouncing on the pattern's red diamonds.

Someday you'll be an adult who brings ice to her own hotel room. What will it feel like to come back to your private bed? You'll lie on the sperm comforter, wedge the dirty sham pillows between your thighs. You picture your adult self: her hips swaying, her helium tits bobbing, a feline smirk splashed across her lips. You'll be bringing back ice to your lover, Dr. Bob, who'll age into craggier perfection. *On your knees, Frankie,* he'll say. *Show me that butt.* And you'll face the headboard and tip your neck as he slides an ice cube up your spine to your brain stem, erasing every last thought.

"Why do you think McDonald's makes Dad poop?" Lawrence says.

You stop.

"You guys ate lunch?"

"Dad and I did. Mom stole some fries."

Inside the stairwell, shiny white paint coats the walls and railings. Lawrence climbs backward. The floor is bouncy like the school gym.

"Lawr, that's effed." Your voice echoes. "Why didn't anyone wake me up? Seriously—Mom and Dad are asking for me to be crazy about, like, everything."

Your brother brings both feet to each step before continuing. He is small for his age, the shortest kid in his grade, yet his eyes look so adult now that they spook you.

"Are you hungry?" He presses the clunky watch that overwhelms his wrist, like the right sequence of buttons might give you superhero powers to eat without getting fat.

You shrug. Yes. No. Yes. Yes. You'd eat an entire bag of chips, a large order of fries, a box of Popsicles.… .

"I'm fine."

You return to the hallway. As you walk, your footsteps fade, the way a vacuum's route vanishes. All traces of you are gone—this might be what it would be like to be totally grown up: you remember you covered familiar ground, but you can't see where or when or how.

You really are hungry. You would eat garbage. You scan for room service leftovers.

The ice machine is in an alcove next to a vending machine. Behind the plastic, gripped by metal springs, the snacks look fake, like the hollow brown chicken drumstick in Lawrence's Fisher-Price kitchen set that you tried to convince him to eat. That wasn't on the list, but it could be.

Lawrence touches your arm. "I've got a dollar. I wouldn't tell."

His bill is rumpled and soft, like the inside of a pocket. He holds out his hand.

You remember his hand when it was the size of a strawberry. You remember him coming home from the hospital, blue and terry-clothed. You were not so bad. You didn't crush his baby fingers in mercy.

"Keep your money. I'll do what Mom does. Ice, ice, baby."

The ice machine grumbles so loud, you and Lawrence laugh. When the ice cubes reach the brim, you take one, pop it in your mouth, and crunch.

#

That night, the salad bar at the Packinghouse fills a wagon, a replica of a Conestoga. You dribble blue cheese dressing on a plate and lick it off your pinky. Your mom picks mandarin oranges from a vat of Hawaiian salad.

"I'll have another lager," your dad says to the waitress.

"What does that taste like?" you ask. "Can I try?"

Your mom sends telepathic brain waves: *lemon water, lemon water, lemon water.*

"Well, the Point is a pilsner. The nose is hoppy.... Do you know what hops are?"

You feel your brain wandering off, heading to a square dance. Why can't you listen to your dad? You see how happy he is to explain.

"Okay, so otherwise it's really mild. Some might call it weak. To tell you the truth, it's not great, but they've made it like an hour from here since the 1800s."

Your mom: "Frankie, think of beer as liquid fat."

Under the table, you kick Lawrence's calf. *See?* You hope he'll speak up—he's little enough to blurt without being "mouthy"—but he plays dumb. He's stacking butters.

The waitress arrives with a rolling wooden cart. For your brother, Buffalo Chicken Tenders and ketchup. A bison burger and Home-on-the-Range Fries for your dad. Your mom ordered for both of you: two Old World Shrimp Scampis, hold the pasta, extra veg.

"So," says your mom. "What's tomorrow's game plan, Novics?"

You played a round of minigolf before dinner, which she effortlessly won. "Diane the Dynamo," your dad dubbed her. Now she sips white wine and saws tails off shrimp with the smugness of a lifelong victor. Her nose is mushroom shaped. Otherwise, she's perfect.

"Water park in the morning, duck tour in the afternoon?" says your dad. He fork-and-knifes his burger, stacking each bite with just one cube of Home-on-the-Range Fries and a dab of ketchup. "The forecast is eighties, sunny, but we could try something—rent a paddleboat, a pontoon. See the rock formations over by Ishnala, out on Mirror Lake. There's a Frank Lloyd Wright house out there. God, for years that place was overgrown. You remember, Di—when we swam out, ditched my mom and dad, summer after college?"

"Mmhmm." Your mom's throat looks like a flower stem when she swallows. "Frankie, please—chew your food," she says.

How can you love her and hate her in back-to-back bites?

"What's wrong with how I'm eating?"

"It's not a race. Your body needs twenty minutes to register fullness."

"Not mine. I know I'm still hungry." You had five shrimp; now you have a plate with an oily pool and parsley, and a new item on the list: *instigates arguments with D.*

Your dad grins like a goof. "Tomorrow, then? What's our decision?"

"I like the duck tour," Lawrence says.

"We do ducks every year. It's always the same! 'Welcome aboard, here's your quacker. Let's hear those honks! What do you call a duck on land? A sitting duck. What's a Wisconsin duck's favorite snack? Cheese curds and *quackers*.'"

"What do you call a bad sport named Francesca?" Your mom's tongue wets her lips. "*Quacked* up."

#

After dinner, back at the Rio Grande, lights out, a blockade of pillows separating Lawrence's half of the bed from yours, you listen to your dad's gargly snore. Moon rays bathe your face. The room is too warm. Behind your knees is sweaty. You can't get out of bed with everyone there. You picture the dense lace of stars, jam your face into the pillow, and hold your breath.

Someday, you want to forget your only friend before Michelle, Monica Bliss, whose father shot himself in the head while his daughters and you watched the pet parade. You were six, focused on the vanilla Tootsie Rolls. You want to forget suicide happened in small houses with pale-green garage doors. You pray to forget the time your father told you that you smelled like a foot. You pray to forget the time you put a rock in Lawrence's soup, the time you swapped his soy milk with half-and-half just to see what would happen (vom). To forget rifling through your mom's closet before your birthday, finding a bag of clothes, and then, on the morning you turned twelve, having only an envelope to open, with a brand-new gym-membership card. You pray to forget finding the list in your dad's cell phone

150

while you waited in the car and he went inside to get your mom's Sunday cappuccino, on a dad-daughter date.

If only you could forget everything, you wouldn't have anything to accidentally tell the shrink.

Because more than anything, you pray to forget two months ago, this season of swimming, the first week, which ruined everything. You kept bumping into Amy Doulas's toe during free sets. First she called you a lesbian and then she accused you of being a molester and then she told you she'd have her father sue you for emotional damage. Then, deliberately, you slo-mo flip-turned, used maximum force to push off against her chest. Toffee-skinned Ravi, the dive coach, had to give her CPR, and luckily she didn't remember what had happened in the seconds before her blackout. *Fuck me,* you thought. *Fuck her. Fuck them all.* That's when you started showering nude.

#

"Good morning, sleepyheads." Pulled back in a tight ponytail, your mom's blond hair is seal sleek; her legs are pliers in yoga pants. Your thighs are blubbery.

"Babe," your dad says, rolling over. On his stomach, he doesn't have a belly. "How late did we sleep?"

"Eight, and I'd say let's get a move on. You guys better be ready for some heat!"

In the bathroom, you change into your team swimsuit. A neon-orange tidal wave stretches across your stomach. Your breasts tug the neck low. You pout at your reflection, tongue around your mouth. Then, in the mirror, you see it. Flesh where there shouldn't be flesh. Not cleavage: side boob.

There is a knock.

The side boob isn't supple like the front of your breasts or puffy like your nipples. It's colder, paler than the rest of you, dead flesh. You pull the suit aside; the side boob hangs like a flap. You try to tuck it in, but the side boob refuses to stay within the fabric.

"Frankie," your mom says, rapping on the door. "Let me see you."

She's already in her black one-piece. Her face is radiant, the apples of her cheeks naturally red violet. She looks at you like you're one more germy pillow on the bed, a germy pillow that needs to get back in the bathroom.

"Do you want to wear one of your dad's T-shirts?" she says.

You try not to watch yourself talking in the mirror. "This isn't *Heavyweights,*" you say.

"Well, you can't go exposing yourself, Frankie."

"Why? We don't know these people."

"Exactly. Have some self-respect."

#

During adult swim, you watch adults wade into the water, slowly, like it is boiling syrup. The women keep their sunglasses on. The men have chests. "Christmas in July" is today's theme, according to the cabana deejay. Every hour, on the hour, he plays "Feliz Navidad."

For these fifteen minutes, you are in charge of Lawrence. He sits next to you, tunneling a finger into his ear. Watery redness washes his eyes, and when he coughs his wussy chest shivers. You want to thump it, hear his empty sound.

"Look at Mom and Dad."

When they aren't across the table, you do love them: your

dad, wearing his father's gold crucifix, floating on his back and disappearing underwater to tickle your mom; and your mom, laughing to captivate him, like she's never had one bad thought.

You sigh. "They're so in love."

"Can I go to the cactuses? That's open for kids."

"Cac-*ti*. And isn't that for babies?" In the cactus grove, mothers in skirted swimsuits lead water-winged toddlers through the streams spurting from plastic plants.

"Come with, Frankie. Don't be dumb."

"I'm not dumb. I'm resting. You go. I'll watch."

Your brother dashes off. You roll over onto your belly. Your skin is slimy from sunscreen. You remember other summers, without lists. You two dove for glow-in-the-dark water rings, snapped Airheads back and forth until the candy shrunk.

Lawrence runs to a cactus, perches on the jet of water, and jumps.

"Frankie," he yells. "I stop it with my butt!"

"¡Cinco, cuatro, tres, dos, uno!" says the deejay. Children bombard the pools, and "La Bamba" begins again.

Your mom slinks toward you. A shrubby-haired lifeguard, probably a couple grades older than you, checks her out.

"Where's your towel, Francesca?" Hers is wrapped twice around her body, knotted sarong-style at her waist.

"In the hampers?"

She frowns.

"I'm tanning."

"There are kids at this pool."

"You think?"

"Francesca, do you need to be argumentative?"

You flip over, prop yourself onto your elbows, and arch your back. You thrust your boobs. *That's it,* says Dr. Bob. *Show those vacation dads!* You tip your head skyward, your eyes looking so far back that you can see the jagged overhang of your own eyebrows. *Provokes family members without reason.* Your mom—her chubby nose, her hacksaw collarbones—can bite you.

#

"Francesca. I'm going to ask you one more time, and then we're packing up. Done. Going home. And we're headed straight to that appointment. ASAP. Not two days from now. Tell me what you did. What did you do to your brother?"

"What did I do?" Your voice gets higher and louder. "How should I know? Why do you think I'd hurt my own brother? C'mon.... Say something!"

Your mother scowls and scowls and scowls.

While you were at the pool, housekeeping remade the room. You sit on the filthy Navajo comforter while your mom stands at the foot of her bed, feet wide, the ready position you crouch into on the block. When she's angry, your mom's features aren't striking. They're stern, carved out, and she's wet, haggard, stringy arms folded across her chest like twine.

Slopping, gaseous dumps blast through the walls: you hear. Your dad, who's been in there with Lawrence, has emerged to say, eyes on the carpet, "Watery stool, explosive."

The room reeks.

"I don't have anything to say to you," your mom says finally.

"Why is everything always on me? Maybe he drank milk!" You pull a loose thread in the hem of the bedspread; alone, you'd tear it with your teeth. "Why is his diarrhea my fault?"

"Diane!" your dad calls.

Your mom is so squeamish, she didn't breastfeed. She takes two backward steps toward the bathroom.

"He gave himself an enema!" Your dad sounds impressed. "You know those cactus shooters! Lare! Little dude! You're in for a rough afternoon."

"Jeremy, it's not funny. Is he going to be okay? Should we go to a hospital?"

"We're good, Di." Your dad comes out of the bathroom and wraps his arms around her, rubbing wings across her shoulder blades. She rests her head on his flubby chest.

"Hey—why don't you girls take off for the afternoon? This has to run its course. No use you holing up. Have fun!"

You consult Dr. Bob. He's hornier than ever. *Frankie, open wide.* In this situation, he finds generosity sexy. Selflessness, a turn on. Isn't that the principle behind giving it up?

"C'mon, Mom." You take a deep breath of charity. "Let's go, me and you."

#

Driving down River Road, you and your mom don't salute Loots. The sign's hieroglyphics dissolve in the rearview. You sit in your dad's spot.

Your mom clenches the wheel. Her thinness makes her transparent: the grit of teeth through her cheeks, the sallow peaks of her knuckles. You see everything about her, how relentlessly she tries, supergluing a smile on her face, striving to be a perfect mom-shaped robot whose affection appears as infrequently as Shilpan's penis, which he withholds, always, waiting for you to give him more, turn around, touch your tits, spank yourself.

You breathe. You feel . . . well. All right.

You pass marinas. The dinky River Road Motel, with its sad swing sets and sandboxes in the front yard. You decide something, once and for all: you aren't afraid of talking to Dr. Rosen or whatever shrink comes next. There will be more. Men in chairs in offices. Bring them on. You will lie. You will do whatever you must to keep yourself yourself. You will say you *don't* want to tweeze the hair off your body. You will say showering naked *does* make you an exhibitionist. You won't mention Amy Doulas. You won't mention Third Eye Blind or the Internet or Shilpan or Dr. Bob or the school bathrooms. You don't need therapy: you need space, a family that accepts you—a hefty girl growing into a buxom woman. That's the secret of adulthood: leave your past behind. Soon real lovers, rough, ready men, men manlier than Dr. Bob, will pleasure every inch of you, curves and rolls and dimples, all the fun filth between your thighs. Your body doesn't belong to your parents or your brother or a therapist: it's yours.

"Strip traffic sucks." Your mom's ponytail is low on her neck. With mussed hair, she looks like a mom.

With you, you realize, she might always be Mom—never Diane.

"It's giving me a stomachache, too," you say. "Stop and start, stop and start."

"What did I tell you about hotel scrambled eggs?"

"I had an omelet."

"Oh . . . that's right."

"With veggies." *Broccoli!* You want to shout, but your mom's chin is puckered; she's about to cry. "Lare will be okay. Dad'll take care of him. He has Gatorade in the cooler."

"I try," your mom says. "I really try."

The Egg turns onto the strip. Here is what you missed yesterday: duck tours, Wax World, Haunted Trails, Pirate's Cove, Feed and Pet the Deer. Corny Maze, Family Land, Noah's Ark, Wonder Spot. Maple fudge and saltwater taffy. A&W. KFC. Culver's. Zinke's, the only grocery store. Tommy Bartlett. Moccasins, temporary tattoos, airbrushed fanny packs, lanyards, key chains, muscle shirts, tomahawks.

There's an open parking spot on Broadway, the main drag. Your mom angles in. The world is wild outside the Rio Grande. The thought is real and stupid—what is this, stranger danger?———but true, because there are so many people— in so many kinds of shorts—flooding the sidewalk that it's overwhelming. For a sec, you envision the Egg backing up and driving to the interstate, you and your mom, ditching the men.

"Let's walk," your mom says.

"For what?"

"… for walking? Walking to walk. Try it, Francesca. Good for the mind and the quads."

At J. T. Buckley's Photo, kids with retainers and polycarbonate glasses try to keep straight faces in costume overcoats and hoopskirts and sausage curls. You flash a jealous smile at them through the window.

"Lice," your mom says. "I see your eyes on those wigs."

A shop that sells only baseball hats. Twenty-four colors of spray-flavored popcorn. Dream catchers with the Chicago Bears logo woven in blue and orange crystals. At the box office for Ghouls of Lake Delton, a line of people snakes around itself: parents flapping brochures, kids chewing glow sticks. You pause at Marge's Sundry Shoppe. Cheese curds?

"Give it up, Frankie. You'll thank me one day for everything decent about your skin."

"Why?"

"Because dairy is a poison that our government subsidizes out the—"

"It's on the food pyramid."

"Sweetheart. Don't be gullible."

Wax World it is.

The entrance takes you through a heavy burgundy curtain. Inside is a mash-up of a museum and a dungeon and a haunted house, how you imagine strip clubs. Men have sex with blow-up dolls: What about with wax? Everything smells like pee and 7 Up and cherry Life Savers: cloying and good.

Your mom tromps up a ramp, through a medieval door, toward a muffled sound. The first exhibit is Rock and Roll. The statues are as real as corpses—at least your grandpa's, the only dead person you've seen. His corpse wasn't him—he was over-rouged, friendly, not his usual gruff firefighter self. Here at Wax World, each figure is almost lifelike, except for a cheery flush in the cheeks, a dumb beadiness in the pupils.

"The Monkees!" For the first time since she sank a putt in the windmill at minigolf, she sounds elated; she shimmies her hips to "Daydream Believer" playing from an orange stage. "I *loved* them! Did you know? Would you believe *your* mom wrote a letter to *the* Davy Jones? He was my junior high crush."

Mr. Jones, you think, meet Dr. Bob. You imagine sliding into a time machine, a funicular like the one your family piled into to see Witches Gulch: Would you and your thirteen-year-old mom be friends? Or would she pariah you like Amy Doulas?

In the Ole Opry section, your mom scowls at a blond in a blue rhinestoned pantsuit. "Dolly Parton. Looks like her waist's life-size."

"How does she stand up?" you say. "With that rack?"

"Frankie!"

Except for Ringo, the Beatles are as expressive as toasters. Elvis molded into an avocado love seat aims a shotgun at a smoking Zenith. Zirconia wink on Michael Jackson's glove.

You push through a red velvet curtain into Old Hollywood. Inside a big video camera like the one your parents used to set up on Christmas, a reel ticks.

"Frankie, my dear, I don't give a damn," your mom says. You smile. She smiles. Maybe, maybe, you are on the same team.

You inch through movies. What will you do if you see Bill Murray? You imagine leaping the velvet ropes, humping frantically, grinding, the way you weren't allowed to at swim team preteen parties.

Frankie, Frankie, Frankie. Show me Shilpan's secret sauce, Dr. Bob whispers.

Shut up, you think. What if he melted? If you toppled him with thrusts? *Don't be here.*

He isn't. Instead of Bill Murray, three John Travoltas cock their cleft chins: one leathered from *Grease,* one in *Saturday Night Fever* disco garb, one from *Pulp Fiction,* a film you weren't allowed to see.

"Marilyn!" you gasp. Stunning women always captivate you. You're surprised by the soul in zombie Norma Jeane. Her eyes are needy and sad. She presses her white dress; a gust blusters through an air vent. Her cleavage rounds beyond her halter: utterly sexy side boob. "She's beautiful."

Your mom sniffs. Her gaze finds the ceiling, which billows with black fabric. "If you like girls like that, Frankie."

"Like what?"

Your mom's eyes trace the blinking white lights outlining the exhibit, up ahead, to the macaroni-and-cheese-colored yellow brick road. You still have Americana (Presidents and Politics). You still have Circus Freaks. Jungle Fever. Oriental Express. Wildly Wild West. Tales from the Crypt.

"Like what?" you say. You set a hand on your waist and grip your flesh. There's plenty of it. You have ample skin. Protection. "Don't ignore me. If I like women like what?"

"If you like girls, angel." Your mom gives you a look like a nudge. "Like Amy?"

"Because because because because because—because of the wonderful things he does!" sings a tinny, analogue, sugary bow-and-arrow soaring through Wax World. Families have been here—you can tell by the ground, the Now and Later-wrapper confetti. Little kids. Velcroed to parents. Juicy Juice mouths and cotton candy fingers. Unconditional love.

"What about Amy? Who told you about Amy Doulas?"

She looks shocked. "Francesca. Why do you think your father and I want you to see a therapist? You're acting out, and . . . we think it's because there's something . . . something sexual you're trying to suppress. To hide. Or express. We *did* know."

"You think I'm a lesbian? Do you even ever pay attention to me?"

"No, honey, we—you're a bright girl: you shouldn't be in some closet."

You walk. Then you run—past Indiana Jones clutching a

coil of rope; past chattery chimpanzees playing against a desert backdrop painted with a fire-red pyramid, the site of virgin sacrifice; past a pair of toddlers hiding behind their unremarkable mother, who scoots them back to Oz as you charge out of Wax World.

Your mom follows you onto the strip. She is fleet and fragile. Her bones blink like cursors in the sudden daylight. She puts her cold hand on you, and her touch is as tickly and awful as the ostrich-feather duster she hands you before Christmas company comes over. You yank away, and she tries to keep hold of you, and you draw your shoulder back like you're about to do freestyle, and you push her, hard, and she staggers backward, into a wide peach-haired man in a sleeveless sweatshirt emblazoned with the Snickers logo.

"Don't touch me, cum bucket!" you scream. The man's pockmarked face is scared. You point at him. "Trash!"

"Francesca!" she says. Her eyes bug, aquamarine and freakish. She's breathless. "What are you . . . we . . . want to make sure you're performing your orientation . . . in appropriate ways. If you're confused, you don't always know—I care about you, and I want to make sure whatever's on your mind gets out in the open while you're still a normal, healthy girl. Francesca, please—you don't need to take this out—"

Done is done. You dart into a crosswalk and run. It's so much harder than swimming. Air is all around you. You don't have to gulp—but you still do. You gulp for a breath. You're sprinting down Broadway, fast—maybe faster than your mother. You skirt crowds of sweating laughing gawking sniffling coughing eating kissing tourists under the fat Wisconsin sun, heavy and hot love all around, the sidewalk jammed with vacationers in tank tops, swim trunks, flip-flops, baseball hats, caramel-colored women in stringy Day-Glo bikinis.

#

Dr. Bob massages your temples as you sit on the pot at Zinke's, the only grocery store in the downtown Dells.

Let it out, sugar cheeks. You did good. One hundred percent grown-ass, he says. *Emphasis on the ass-isis.*

You don't have change for a pay phone. No school ID or library card. You and the Egg are through. This is the toilet at the market where your family has bought plastic silverware and smushy white bread and Peter Pan peanut butter for day-trip sandwiches. Behind the deli counter, across from a break room blaring Rick Springfield, in a bathroom with a checklist and a blue ballpoint dangling from the door, you try to forget your parents and Lawrence, "cut ties" with lies that might be trying to find you, lies waiting for you to eat dinner and lose at mini-golf and slumber beneath Rio Grande germs.

Whatever, family. On the pot you spread your legs. You squeeze a fistful of flesh on your thighs, fulvous from the sun. The burn hurts. A giant water blister will cover it. A skin sheet. A liquid pouch. It will be disgusting and fragile. Satisfying to peel off.

Your fingers spider-walk over your labia. Inside, the skin is hot and moist and red and pebbly, a gross-out exhibit in the children's zoo. In shampoo commercials, orgasmic pleasure is an ice cream sundae, a hair toss, a rain forest beating with quetzals and waterfalls and Spanish orchids. Your pleasure, when it comes, and it will come, will smell like Zinke's: potato salad and lunch meat, Daisy bologna.

My behemoth, Dr. Bob whispers as you stroke yourself. *My Amazon, my Xena.* You picture your mother, like a leopard or a panther, sleek and dazzled with dewdrops, bounding through the rain forest, swinging from vines, her triceps stapled with muscle. She is looking for you, calling for you, asking the fuchsia flowers and the mossy stones and the braided roots and the three-toed sloths if they've seen you, if they've heard your Frankie footfalls. But you're sneaky, a swimmer, lithe in liquids. There are rivers and lakes and lagoons, coves your mother's never seen—cold, dark whirlpools where you can be a friend to the minnows and lesser fish.

Anniversary

They ran along the lake and, spent, heaving, beating, breath-less, fucked. A mirror on the wall: grace wasn't in her. She wasn't on a ceiling, a fireplace, a rug. To stay present, she tried not to overstare at her face. She glued her chin to her chest and watched him enter her again and again until pleasure was immediate, imminent, instant. No. They washed each other. Rose petals sloughed off the soap and dissolved on their soft stomachs.

From the street, the restaurant looked deserted. Graffi-ti sliced across the awnings. Charlie bought two bottles of wine, and they ate cobia and cow tongue, heart and ravioli pumped with truffle and yolk. No waiters—four chefs took turns serving. Charlie wanted pictures; she'd left the camera in the room. Sweetbreads with lambic, jellyfish with Gewürz-traminer, and, halfway through the tasting, Bianca needed to pee.

"Is there a bathroom?" she asked a chef who came to take their plates.

No, he told her. She recognized his face from pages, places. He was in charge, owner and executive chef; he was young and brazen and wild and damaged; his stare didn't stare.

"We use the alley."

His stare didn't straighten.

"C'mon. Through the kitchen."

She wandered, hungry. She followed him and palmed a freezer.

"Watch the step," he said. Now he was one of four men, each grimier than the last.

She always got drunk off champagne. While she peed, she tried to make out the chefs: they knifed and spoke. They were men and, over speakers, they piped hip-hop into the restaurant, music her husband recognized. He could identify songs by year and producer; oh, he'd unscrambled a brainteaser. Answers didn't make you anyone better. Bianca was younger.

She heard pounding and a chain. She washed her hands, and her face lingered over the sink. The light in the bathroom came out red. Bianca lifted her dress and stared at her thighs: black lace held her up, and tomorrow it'd be useless, the feeling in her legs eviscerated. She wished. They'd eaten six courses. Seven plus amuse. Impossible to know what the chefs said but she could picture them, the executive chef with his oily hair, his rehab bloat, his heart a muscle quartered on a greasy plate, his ear against the door.

Radiant Spiritual Being

At the red gate, the massage therapist wrote in the first message. After no answer: *I think this is you?*

In bed, surrounded by the morning's work—corsages of crumpled tissue, coconut crumbs—the phone chimed again. Quit it, Layla hissed, eyeing the bassinet.

It was a pill-shaped piece of furniture. The base was mahogany, and the sides were bone mesh. Its thin legs were bent, scalene rabbit-ear antennas. The design sedately nodded toward mid-century, a "smart" sleeper: an algorithm, a subaudible motor, a sensor that would discern baby cries from background noise. Layla kept the bassinet unplugged.

It was a season of fires. They radiated out from Los Angeles, blasting through the Hills, and last night one had overtaken the Catholic college where Layla taught. Her students, girls shawled in blankets, hugging their backpacks marsupially, were evacuated by ambulance and Mercedes van. She was their chic-aunt professor, they trusted her with their truth, and they were flooding the class discussion board with videos of the 405 sky bleeding out, streaky, dirt-red apocalypse.

Here ?? a new message read.

She took a small brown envelope from under the pillow. Yesterday it had contained six raw CBD macarons; today there was one. But classes were canceled. The universe of California was giving her a pass, pardoning her 660 stoner calories. She put the macaron in her mouth, crumpling the envelope, bonbonnière of the cannabis age. She'd used the word bonbon in a lecture, once, and been met with blankness. Bon, as in good, she'd said, like . . . that good-good.

Layla wobbled over to the bassinet. She touched the mesh and straightened the swaddle spread out on the thin mattress, a pouch of stretchy fabric printed with madly smiling daisies. Her neighbor's bird often caused the sensor to misfire, triggering a broken, brutal rocking.

\#

Outside, the courtyard was hazed in opalescent light. Under the fermented tang of figs, sour red queens that fell from the mammoth Moreton Bay, the air stunk of smoke. Thirty miles away last week, fifteen this morning. The closer the fires, the less they bothered her.

She squinted against the high eastern sun. Behind the fence, a woman in compression tights and a top with a mandarin collar waved.

"I heard your shoes, mama," the woman said, grinning at Layla's velveteen mules. The woman dropped her phone into a tote, where a bolster stuck up like an enormous baguette.

She introduced herself as Beri, short for Bernice, Beri Yawn. "How's the morning going?" Beri asked, glancing around the courtyard. An armless Venus, the sooty bin of a grill. A glitter of hummingbirds above the hedges, floating birthstones, too light to leave a shadow.

Layla exhaled.

"The world is crazy right now," Beri said. "Good for you for making time for yourself with all this. How's the baby doing?"

Layla kinked an eyebrow behind a pair of Prada sunglasses from a few seasons back, when she and the world had had more levity, when fashion could still be arch. If now were then, the frames would be perfect: chunky, jagged flames.

"I'm this way."

She decided to say nothing as much as possible. If she was tempted to talk, she'd eat the camellia oil from her lipstick. She had gotten dressed today, every day this week. Short black tulip skirt, gold Calyce clip-ons, glamorous house shoes. She put on makeup. She was a woman who valued self-maintenance, who believed tiny luxuries might save her. That woman had booked a treatment, a postpartum womb massage. Beneath her mules, the figs flattened into teardrops, smashed open and purple, exposing their withered seeds.

#

Relax, Beri insisted, she'd call if she needed anything, but Layla hovered over the bassinet, half-monitoring the preparations.

Beri was sporty, color-blocked—purple-tipped ponytail, dense white polish on her toes—and she moved swiftly. She turned on a portable speaker, set a jar candle on the nightstand, and out of the bag came the bolster, a folded white sheet, a deep blue towel.

"Do you have a lighter?" Beri asked, testing a pillow, one of the firm ones that Layla had splurged on for Dom's (canceled) visit. "I used my last match."

In the kitchen, Layla opened a drawer. She gazed out the window at her neighbor's tile-roofed mansion, the secluded in-law casita behind the patio sprouting with a family of green garden umbrellas. Her apartment was small. Not awful for Los Angeles. Fine for her and a newborn. A one-year-old. Even a toddler, maybe. And the views, bubblegum jasmine and bamboo her neighbor nurtured. He was a beautiful man with a lovely, hopscotching accent, a rich Cuban teddy bear with fabulous shoes. Plus, the bird. Layla had never seen the bird, but she imagined its celadon feathers, its canny eye, bloodshot from smoke, sizing her up from its invisible perch. It watched her test the lighter, squawking its catcall: *wee woooo.*

"Did I mention how amazing you look?" Beri said when Layla came back. "Honestly, I couldn't even tell that you just had a baby. That's hard work, mama!"

Layla frowned. "I used to be a gymnast. And I did hot yoga—"

"My mother made me do gymnastics," Beri said, smoothing a wooly blanket over the sheet. "Even though I was absolutely terrible at it and basically born with the wrong body, according to my Chinese mother. By the time I was nine, I was, say, five-one. One hundred and twelve pounds? Or maybe one hundred and five? Not huge, but the other girls were these seventy-pounds sprites. Um, no. The whole sport is one big anorexia incinerator."

"Incubator?" Layla said.

She could never imagine imposing anything like that on her daughter, Beri said. James, she told Layla, will be one next week, and she's such a tomboy, so rough and tumble even though she was born at twenty-eight weeks and spent her first three months in the NICU.

"With a needle in her skull," Beri said, lighting the candle. French vanilla bloomed. "My partner and I had to literally advocate for her to be fed. The nurses in the NICU were withholding. How messed up is that?"

Nick-U, Nick-U. Layla had never heard the word spoken, had only read it in tiny font truckled by video ads on her phone in this bed, and it hung before her like a hologram, a door to another room. Edibles messed her up. She was queasy. The macaron was still in her throat, a clot of oily, salty coconut. She bit her tongue and felt herself float off, like a syllable.

"So," she heard Beri ask. "Where's the little nugget?"

#

All choices are bad choices in love, Layla would say, bad romance, she said in her Deviant Women classroom, blackboards iced over with sliding dry erase panels, plagiarizing Proust and Lady Gaga, both ancient history to eighteen-year-old girls.

The trope of the chance meeting.

Love at first sight?

Think about it.

She would stare off out the window, stretching a minute into eternity, gazing at the confused blue horizon, where the Pacific Ocean seeped into the sky. When there were choices in a relationship, she said, they could only be bad because it meant the socialized mind, the rationale mind, your mind governed by fear and logic and buy-buy-buy, white-picket values, your mind had won at the expense of your heart, that boiling hopeful organ. The girls blinked at her skinny thighs, mottled skin peeking through the fishnets, each gap in the stockings a new question: Do you have a boyfriend? Are you married? Do you have kids? They were most curious at the start of the semester, when she told them they could ask her anything.

-Thirty-nine. Yes. Thank you. I work hard.

-Handstands.

-A chile relleno burrito. From La Azteca—.

-Boot shopping with Madonna.

She had met Dom over Labor Day weekend, two weeks into the term. Her students knew nothing of Chicago. She'd forgotten to pack underwear and bought herself a seven-pack from the Girls department at Target, Days of the Week. When she'd swiped right wearing Tuesday, cotton-candy pink, dizzy-eyed unicorns, she was on Roosevelt Road, mouth frozen and red from Morello cherry ice, sun-blissed and kissing the arm of an impossible bookish king of the Gold Coast, staggering back to his soaking tub, his bed, between fucks five and six getting herself the wettest she'd be all the livelong weekend ogling his bookshelf. He had a degree from U of C, translated Italian folktales and poetry, mainly the hard labors of Pavese for fun—bahaha. He collected dictionaries. She took down two and opened them on his desk. She had one hand over *cloaca* and the other on *keime* when he came so hard the condom broke.

#

She floated back. Curtains pulled shut. Bed covered by white sheet. Vanilla candle burning.

"Ready when you are," Beri said. It was a deep, athletic voice, the voice of a woman with strong hands. "Keep your underwear on, bra optional—it's nice if you're leaking."

Layla stepped out of her mules and shortened by an inch. She unclasped her skirt. She left on the ratty lavender sports bra she wore for Bikram.

"Careful getting on the bed," Beri said. "Are you sore?"

Awkwardly, as though horizontally jumping a hurdle, she laid herself down. Did Beri notice her hammerhead hip bones? Once Dom had come between them, that dip below her navel he called la fossa. Touchdown! she'd crowed, so high off gummies and ardor that everything she said seemed brilliant, nine times in a row brilliant, how do you radio silence someone worth fucking nine times in twenty-seven hours? An hour or five bags of macarons, four tubes of Melrose lipstick, one-third a haircut, one month at her yoga studio, one-seventh her rent, half a flight to Chicago; one one-hundredth the cost of freezing her eggs, round two.

"I'm going to put on the eye pillow now," Beri said. "And a towel to protect your hair from the oil."

She gathered Layla's hair and turbaned the towel. The eye pillow was snug, eucalyptus-scented silk filled with tiny beads.

"Deep breath in," Beri said. Her palms pressed on Layla's shoulders. "And out." There was a heavy touch on the ball of her left shoulder. A pause. For a moment, she only heard the thrum of the ceiling fan, its dust-furred blades churning smog and spindly-legged mosquitos that squeezed in through the gaping screens. Then, over the speaker, a muted chant and an echoing bell. The pump of lotion. Beri kneaded, working the moist slop over her sinuous bicep. Down, tracing around her elbow, the knobby point, the inside, a pond of flesh marked with good veins.

One by one, Beri tugged her fingers. The pinky and thumb knuckles cracked.

"Relax," Beri whispered. She picked up Layla's arm and shook it like a useless tube. "I know it's hard, mama. Relax."

She covered her left arm with the wooly blanket and changed the music. Behind the eye pillow, Layla blinked. *Wee wooo.* Outside, a woman yelled, *Tamales!* Layla pictured her north of the courtyard, far from the Cuban teddy bear's dollhouse of umbrellas, pushing a shopping cart filled with tamales all papoosed on a bed of newspaper.

That's what people said, and Layla had never seen it, but she believed it. She was trying.

She tried to picture the woman's cart, a stroller of banana leaves and corn husks. She tried to tune out the bird. She tried to breathe as Beri reached under her neck, scrabbling and burrowing like a badger, smooth, powerful strokes. Scooping and curing the muscle. Kneading the knotty rosettes from her back.

"I'll begin the meditation now," Beri said. "We'll finish your legs and then work on your belly."

Wee woooo.

Beri lifted the blanket and began rubbing her right thigh, doughy, where every ounce of her eight pregnancy pounds had settled.

The audio shifted, and a man began speaking in a careful, tranquil tone. He introduced himself—he was a prominent guru, and Layla recognized his name, even though she did not subscribe to wellness or spiritual anything. She was vanity healthy. She had a better metabolism than she cared to admit;

before getting pregnant, she had done yoga to look hot naked and stayed slim on a diet of Luna bars and white wine.

Our cells are constantly eavesdropping on our brains, the guru said. If the brain was sick, the body would manifest that sickness, too. Negativity breeds negativity, the guru said. Our bodies are radiant spiritual beings. They want to be in motion.

Yes. Yes. She wanted to sit up, grab Beri by the wrist, and spin her toward the bassinet. Know anyone that needs this? Pristine. Mint. Un-fucking-used. She wanted to spell it out: D&C. Anoxic uterus. Shove the post-op instructions in her face. She wanted to tell her that Dom wanted nothing to do with her, had refused their child even when there was still the possibility of their child. She wanted to tell her that she could never go back to Chicago and never drink Amaro again and never eat bucatini in bed, bucatini from a basin bowl like in the Nora Ephron movie she never should've watched, not alone with the bird and the bassinet, soaking through diaper-thick pads after the procedure, with ninety-seven papers on Catherine Breillat to grade and her belly still puffy, and she could've been a mother, more than his lover; that part of herself had been writhing, alive, in Dom's anacondan clutches. She'd seen herself making her pretty nails pious in prayer when the priest came to say private Mass in his family's chapel, teaching their child here is the church, here is the steeple, boy, girl—it hadn't mattered, it didn't, it doesn't—there would've been money, so much money that she would've had the time to learn Italian so she could teach their bambino, and Dom would've kept translating folktales: *There once was a fair, lovelorn princess surrounded by flames in not-so-glamorous Los Angeles.*

Wee woooo. Wee woooo. Wee woooo.

Layla winced. She prayed for the bassinet to jolt alive. If it started rocking, she could explain this. But she'd gotten dressed, put on lipstick, double-checked the cord. No misfire. Only a bridge in the guru's meditation, a crescendo of ethereal ambience.

Wee woooo. Wee woooo.

Beri's hands stopped. "That . . . is some bird," she said, laughing shortly.

She snugged the blanket around Layla's legs, tucking under her toes. She sprayed a mist that smelled familiar, like peppermint custard, a candy from her childhood. Layla's heartbeat quickened. She did not like being so alert, blindfolded.

"I know this is what you've been waiting for," Beri said. "It's belly time. Remind me. Were you a vaginal—?"

"Yes."

"How are you healing?"

"Not well, not—it's been a rough few weeks."

"Tell me about it. These are the hardest. You guys sleeping?"

She choked with laughter, too loud, a cocktail shaker full of glass laugh. She laughed a long time. She was infected with laughter; she was so fucking high; that was the only way to work through any of this; she would never stop cracking up, until, of course, she did.

"Okay, I get it," Beri said. "Well, you don't have any rib flaring. Keep breathing, deep belly breaths. I know it's hard, but that'll help as we do this. Ready to go for a ride, mama?"

"Sure."

Sure. Even the nurses had been sure until the second ultrasound showed her empty sac. Follicle, sac. Happy thirty-ninth birthday, Miss New Vocabulary. With the eye pillow on, she was not sure: Had she started crying?

Beri set two hands on the center of Layla's belly. She stretched her fingers, burying each one like Layla's flesh was wet sand. A ballet of concentric circles, spiraling out until she was cupping the sides of her body, the cliff's edge of Layla's ribs.

Layla heard the stubborn sound of a lid. Her stomach felt warm and porous, like a membrane.

"This is all good things," Beri said. "I make this scrub, one hundred percent natural."

It was thick and grainy and smelled of orange spices. Beri painted it all over, drawing great curves with the sides of her hands, smearing it around, reaching under, working on her back, remaking Layla's skeleton. Then she placed what felt like a metal baton between her hip bones, over la fossa, and rolled it up and down her abdomen. Layla tensed.

Wee woooo.

The rolling kept going. Layla clenched her abs and dug her thumbnail into the pad of her index finger.

"Super sensitive, I know," Beri said, softly. "Just try to relax. Just put your mind in a calm place. Think about your daughter. Yeah? Tell me her name."

"Wee wooo," Layla barked. "Wee wooo."

The room was quiet between them. She heard Beri swallow. The hands were radiating toward her center, moving over her abdomen like spokes on a wheel, wiping the scrub, and then Beri plugged a finger in Layla's naval. She held it there. Pressed.

Put your finger in the socket. Stay still.

She felt something unlatching in her throat, a trapdoor opening wider and wider the more Beri plugged, plugged again and again, fucking her belly button with that one finger until Layla jerked up, threw off the eye pillow, and said, "I'm going to be sick."

Beri's eyes went big. "Woah, okay, stopping, mama. Do you—"

She ran into the bathroom and stared at the toilet seat, flecked with soot from the open window. She waited for sickness to erupt. When it didn't, she forced it with two fingers. She vomited the macaron, a coffee she'd forgotten she brewed, a pacifier, a tamale, a wooden Popsicle stick, electric-green feathers. Then nothing but glair, the coating of her stomach.

#

Here is our guiding thought, the guru was saying.

Here. And here. Here.

Layla tasted her mouth. Cherries. Beri paused the speaker.

She stood on the other side of the bed, hands on her waist, mouth pursed. She looked bewildered.

"Has that ever happened to you?" she said. "Do you want to keep going?"

"No," Layla said dryily.

"Good call," Beri said. "Do you want me to make you a cup of tea? I can stay with you until your husband gets home. You said he's walking the baby? Want me to give him a call?"

Layla went over to the bassinet. The daisies grinned, amused by her sulkiness, her posture, her blank stare. "No, I don't."

"Can I bring you anything to eat?"

Tamales, tamales, wee wooo, wee wooo. The Yankee Doodle of a sketchy ice cream truck, the side painted with a cartoon bear saying "Yo quiero" and a cartoon mouse shaking his finger: "No no no."

Beri packed up the towels, the blanket, the sheets, the bolster. She set a sachet of rose tea on the nightstand.

"The candle is yours," she said. "A little you time when baby's asleep."

Layla could tell her eyes were dead. When she had first begun teaching, she had had bad evaluations. She was mean. She was pissy. She was scary, so she changed. She had become someone girls could confide in.

She stood frozen, leaning against the wall, beside the bassinet. Beri looked at her.

"It gets easier. This is a lot. For sure a lot. All those prenatal hormones just shut off like a faucet. They call it a hormonal cliff, what happens after you give birth. From zero to sixty—or sixty to zero. You see what I'm saying?"

"I really don't."

She heard her skinny voice say ciao and Beri's flip-flops smack down the stairs. She sat on the bed, and then she was tired of sitting.

Carefully, cupping the wick, she picked up the candle. The glass jar was hot in her hand. The vanilla was loud and sweet in the small room. It was emptier before. It could be emptier again. *Wee wooo*, the bird's cries slid off the blades of the fan.

For the first months of the baby's life, the bassinet should be free of obstructions. No blankets, no stuffed animals, no pacifiers. In this bassinet, there was only the swaddle. The daisies said look at me. Love me. Layla laid the candle on its side in the cradle. As the flames poured out, she plugged in the cord.

Patient

On Saturday nights, I am haunted by cumbrous memories of my mother. Nine months ago, on these nights, my mother would call from the other side of the country to read me her woes. Her fat Polish fingers would squeeze a juice jar of red wine as she spoke of her muddy yard, her cracked cuticles, shit in the yard, shit on her boots. I was a young wife at the time, walking after supper to help myself digest. What I wanted to digest was a baby. So alone with child, so alone on Saturday night. So cumbrous, my mother.

Now I wander the ward and look for friends or TV. It is not like when the baby was born, pushing him in a plastic bin on a wheeled cart, being stopped to receive a hand massage, a cookie and milk. Here in the promise of health and its lies: snacky self-care is exposed for the rot it is. I am supposed to want arm strength enough to lift my child, the mirage of a robust pulse, a BMI of bright binomials. The tolerance to swallow what I chew.

Luck has her eye on me, and after pacing the corridor a few times I hear faint voices coming from the art room. I follow them. Past the nurses' station, where computers sleep, guarded by a row of nail polish bottles, glittering stuff the staff steals from us. Past the listening library. The door to the art room is barely open.

Baby girl, where is your fear? You could lose visiting privileges, phone privileges, day passes, dinnertime decaf. What sublimity do you seek? You know the art room: construction paper, dull pencils, crayons, markers, glue sticks, *National Geographic* battlements.

Yet, I slip inside. The lights with their saline chill. On TV, a flip-haired actor wrings his leather jacket and paces like a panther. There is an orderly sitting on the couch. Dorota. Dorota tells everyone to call her Dorothy.

She has unlocked the supply cabinet and removed the bin of safety scissors. They have rounded points and squeaky plastic handles the color of 7 UP bottles. Dorota's big blond hair is behaving like a beehive, her breasts are multiparous, her storm-blue nails are round as a pinup's rump.

She is cutting fashion magazines, the ones we're not supposed to see.

This ward is a test with all wrong answers; the scale goes up instead of down. This ward is staffed by people who ooze over fireworks and switch their hips to Fleetwood Mac. They wear scrubs and crosses, and so does Dorota, stalled mid-snip, scissors alligator-mouthed. She gawks at the TV. Her crucifix bobs in her cleavage as she cachinnates over Chandler.

Chandler is locked in a vestibule. He is scrambling and antic, but at least he has gum. Torching seven calories an hour.

Dorota snips around a dress of eel-gray sequins and adds it to the array on the coffee table, next to a barge-sized box of tissues.

She doesn't say anything when I sit down next to her, only twists to hide the inside of the magazine. She licks her finger, the chalky underbelly of a long nail, as she pages. On-screen, the Village is in a blackout; New York is going haywire; the other friends are running out of candles and patience. In our ward, the power is human. The wall vent clears its throat and cycles on the heat. The honeycomb fixtures flicker, and I am strobed by the luminance of caged madness.

"My daughter and I are going shopping," Dorota says during a commercial. "Do you like this?"

She tap-taps the jut of my knee with the green part of the scissors and shows me the dresses. I am nauseated and calmed just seeing them—those girls, those girls, those dresses on girls. They are backless, haltered, sequined pageant styles that skim the models' bodies. The models are thin, but not thin like me, and not thin like the others on the ward, and their flesh is not dry or scaly but tan and moisturized, supple, nubile, luminescent—precious words, words that are supposed to remind me of my baby.

"Pretty," I say. "Very glamorous."

"Very expensive," Dorota says. "But it's a special time. She should enjoy it. I do not want to ruin it for her."

"'Show me the gold tunnel,'" I say. "'Show me where the gold tunnel goes.'"

Dorota's scissors pause.

"It's a Nevada thing," I say. "From the Gold Rush, all right? Don't be scared. I'm all here. I'm with it. I'm fine."

"She is a seal on my heart, a seal of *gold*," Dorota says, peeling back the flap of a Shalimar sample. "You have a child, and you think you know anything about this life? Forget it. You see that gold tunnel you imagine all along, and it is not so easy to find your way. You get lost in the tunnel, no? Even if you do not end up in a place like this."

"You're not lost," I say. "My mother would never have looked for prom dresses for me. My mother called me a—"

"Now, but not always. When my daughter is two, three, I had headaches. Very bad headaches. My husband says I was a demon. I tell you, Joanna, I wanted to smash my head against the wall."

Dorota digs in her pocket, rummaging away the gravity of her admission. And that is how I know she is good. Caring. The kind of mother I've never had and never will be. She does not cavil to emphasize her own suffering. She does not answer "how are you?" with "fine," where fine is a mortal wound. She does slake her thirst to starve and shirk her production of milk. Dorota unwraps a cough drop. On TV, the loft lights flicker in the Village, and the two people with the most voluminous hair are kissing.

"It's almost Sunday," she says. I hear the lozenge clack against her teeth. "I still have to drive home, get home at twelve-thirty, clean up, go to sleep, wake up, make blintzes before church."

I cringe at the old memory of myself, a chunky girl, microwaving eggs into a plasticky omelet for my mother, the horrid smell of zapped Velveeta.

"For my mother, my mother-in-law. We celebrate them, every year. We give them roses, yes, yellow roses." She pauses and then speaks more forcefully. "Don't you have happy memories with your family? Didn't your mother like to cook?"

In the Village, the sarcastic friend has said goodbye to a model future. The heat has cycled off. All the dresses in front of us are the color of deep-water fish or grape soda.

Dorota shakes her head. "I'm sorry. I know. I should keep my beeping mouth shut."

"It's me, Dorothy," I say. "I ate her kluski, her fruit dumplings. I swallowed them. All of it. I swallowed it with bleach."

The credits come in their chatty font. There it is. If you starve yourself, you starve your child. Poison yourself, poison your milk. Midnight.

"I hope you have a beautiful Mother's Day," I say.

"C'mon, mama." Dorota sweeps the gowns into a hospital envelope. "Let's go back. You need your rest. Your little boy is coming tomorrow, yes? Your little one and your husband. I bet they're bringing you flowers. You need flowers in your room."

She flicks the light switch with her thunderhead nails and leads me to my room, pats my bony shoulder, and waves her badge in front of a censor that controls the ward's doors.

Sunday is here. Dorota, buxom, stable, constant, has gone home. My visitors have left me a gasping succulent. Shrimpy, spiny, the color of fatigue. My mother used to send me flowers, back when I was in that pregnant apartment, lush ballets of pink and cream and green and gold, stigma and stem, a bullet or a blade. Every time, the cursive in the card said the same thing: *Do I need a reason to tell you I love you?*

These Things Happen

*H*er name was Althea. When she was fifteen, she hosted Soundtrack Saturdays, and once her cohost, a junior wearing Vans and arms cuffs, stood her by the microphone and knelt under the table, squeezed her birthmarked knee, and ate her out until she came on-air, faking a hiccup before a song by Garbage. When she was younger, Althea's father lavished her with love: he took her to a bookstore by the riverwalk; taught her words like *demilune* and *gallnut;* and whether the gift could be dog-eared or lost in Althea's mouth like milk or mustard, he hugged her. A wry, tonsured man in rectangular glasses, Avery Zafaris's embrace was intentional. He respected her; he loved her.

It started when she was six. Her older brother was already out of the house, at boarding school up north by Lake Michigan. He had left crates of toys: plastic chicken legs, plastic hamburgers; a band of scaly dinosaurs. One morning, Althea's mother found Althea in the den. Posed on the desktop were a stegosaurus, a tyrannosaurus, and two naked dolls between them. The dolls' legs were wrapped in fabric loops from the potholder kit; their wrists, overhead, were also wrapped. Althea's mother scooped up her daughter and boxed her son's toys. Let's play nice, she said, frowning like an owl. Your father has made you so odd. From then on, Evie Leighton-Zafaris spent her free time with her daughter. They did wholesome things, stewed D'Anjous into pear butter or visited the zoo, where they'd nibble animal fries, salty, soft, shaped like sloth bears, which were actual animals, according to placards, only endangered. If you were too strange, too big, too much, watch out—Evie let Althea deduce that. She'd taught grade-school art until her daughter was born, and she still painted fairylands with spires and turrets, vines twisting over castles. They mesmerized Althea. All the dark corners her mother had missed. In a painting outside the bathroom with the Mickey shower curtain, swaths of fog cloaked the walls of a palace, and Althea knew that inside was a dungeon she could only enter with a bloody key. Air sour as boiled eggs. A rank moat swam with bugs. Men dripped molten honey on maidens on the rack, splayed, rag-gagged, gasping for what they craved. Meanwhile, her mother wrote to family, reporting her daughter's precocities: She invented a board game, Cats' Mishaps.

Althea's father was a therapist. Dr. Avery Zafaris was suburban-famous for "The A-Z," a segment he hosted on WGN that demystified raising adolescents. At his office, he forewent lunch, drafting scripts, to free nights and weekends for family. Then he was his inquisitive self, except wittier, flirtful. He picked up a bottle of sauvignon blanc and Thai: fresh spring rolls; two orders of shimmering, oleaginous pad woon sen—his daughter was hooked. He asked her about tests, and indifferent

Althea shared her grades (96, 99), until, finally, kindling her chopsticks, she'd pounce on gossip. In fourth grade, the history teacher hickied Andrea Parsell; in fifth, rat-tailed Zed pinched the choirmaster's nipple. Althea Elaine, please, her mother said. Her father laughed. Imagine if we had a boring kid, he said. She's going to be lonely, Evie said. Hey there lonely girl, Avery sang, and Althea joined him in falsetto.

She was lonely for much of school, only too stubborn to admit it. Boredom was a sign of being boring; loneliness followed the same rule. The summer after eighth grade, Althea's parents enrolled her in day camp by the riverwalk. The camp was called Edgemere, a lush Eden of garths and cloisters behind calligraphic iron gates, perfect for creative starvelings. Three two-week sessions, each devoted to a medium. Photography to start. Althea brought her camera, which, until this summer, had shot aardvarks and ratty little kultarrs in Brookfield's small mammal house. At Edgemere, Althea saw black-and-whites by Ansel Adams and Sally Mann. Learning foreground and background was like uncovering the legend to a map. Your background doesn't disappear, the teacher explained. It's muted. Suppressed.

There had not been girls she got along with at school, but at camp Althea met a waify brunette named Natalie who looked like she'd wandered in from *Oliver Twist*. She had an orphaned, depleted aspect that captivated Althea—ringlets and a pinafore would've suited her, this girl, so yearnful, she'd probably gobble an apple down to the core, seeds and all, even if an orchard grew in her stomach.

They were partnered for the last project: portraits that revealed a biographical truth about the subject. To prepare, they interviewed each other. The teacher provided a list of questions that Natalie used and Althea didn't. It was a green, humid day. The girls sat cross-legged under a magnolia on a damp patch of petals verging on rot. Althea wore khaki shorts and her Edgemere tank. Natalie had on a wrinkly hippie skirt that accentuated her stick legs and a turtleneck under her camp shirt. Somewhere in Naperville, an ambulance howled. Althea asked: Is *Citizen Kane* a film or a movie? What's your favorite holiday? Why are you wearing two shirts? Natalie put down her notebook, stuck her pen in the spiral, and rolled up her sleeves. The rest of her body froze when she showed Althea her forearms. The skin was hairless, skim-milk pale, and rowed with dried-blood slashes, each as long as a stick of gum. Althea nodded; she ran a pinky over the scabs, one by one. They were rough, like stitches in the mended quilt her mother used on picnics. Then sadness hit Althea with such force that her stomach buckled. Natalie had hidden a part of herself that Althea recognized as haunted and real and beautiful. I'll take care of you, she promised silently. She tied a blade of grass in a knot and handed it to Natalie. They had all afternoon. After vegetarian corndogs and pudding in the cafeteria, they went to the prop room, and Althea photographed Natalie with a calico cat, its one whisker kinked into a question mark.

Althea was eighth in a class of 973 her first year in high school. For her stellar GPA, her father bought her a pair of emerald studs that she never took out—she didn't have the seconds to waste. Life possessed the monocular quality of a dash. And then, at the beginning of sophomore year, there was Natalie: her family had moved districts. Her locker was in the C Wing by Althea's, two minutes from the vending machines where Pepsi products were a dollar, and on the way they went by glamour shots of athlete-heroes past—in jerseys, teeny shorts, foot propped on volleyball, elbow on knee, fist under jaw—hissing *we survived*. For once, Althea had a friend. They met at 7:43 a.m., and the rest of the day the two orbited, detouring their routes between classes so they could be together. They drank so much soda, they switched to diet. They talked so close they tasted the aspartame curdling their breath. There was everything to say, and no one before had been right to tell.

Since Edgemere, they had written letters that, on Natalie's end, grew increasingly personal. Her parents were lawyers, "out of the picture" in Natalie's words; she'd spent her childhood with a neighborhood couple who had a tree house for their grandson, Max. He was posset-pallored, with a knack for meanness, Natalie wrote. Not just meanness.

All year Althea and Natalie passed a leopard-fur notebook. It was strokable, cheekable, smotherable. Althea wanted to breathe it in, track Natalie's ruby nail polish streaks, lick the lost molecules of her perfume. It didn't bother Natalie to write about Max; she just didn't want to talk about him. Out loud. She didn't want to pollute the air with his name. She wrote: I am not a victim. These things happen—happened. Much, much, much worse could've gone down. It's not like I'm a misandrist. He had blackmailed her into a game of Truth or Dare that spanned summers, puberty. Dares. Predictable. No one forced me to go to the tree house, she wrote. Fascinated by fluids, he dared her to ingest an array of them, hers, his. Lick this: ice pack (melted), armpit (sweaty), hedgehog (mysteriously damp), belt buckle (gold). What Natalie had endured or enjoyed shifted, but Althea never doubted her. How could she? She kept their correspondence with her Edgemere portfolios in a Marshall Field's box, and whenever she went into the box, she was rocked with ecstasy, routine as the carbonation kiss when you open a soda. The details, she couldn't forget. They popped into her head when she ran laps in gym: He dared me to put a Super Soaker inside me; so, okay. Not okay, Althea insisted, panting the last mile. Fucked. Up. It had happened to Natalie, but Althea was beginning to feel it had happened to her, too. The more she reread the notes, the more the past became hers, a film starring a vaguely pretty any-girl caught in a tree house.

Althea wrote back and told Natalie how much she loved her. How they would go to the same college in Los Angeles and be roommates. They would rent a tiny apartment with only enough room for a queen-size four-post bed, with Velcro handcuffs around one of its posts and a Moulin Rouge mirror and a mini-fridge for Diet Pepsi and whipped cream. They would lure boys into the apartment, boys whose minds they'd blow, boys who'd crawl and beg and weep, who'd buy them fat-free, sugar-free, free, free, free frozen yogurt, with sprinkles, rainbow sprinkles, boys they'd kick out when the sex got old. Strange sensations met Althea when she described this future. She felt disembodied. Heard a ringing in her right ear. Saw peripheral shimmers. Head light as a balloon, she felt as though she were sprinting toward an invisible finish line, sitting in Trig/Pre Calc, watching triangle-haired Miss Stickman solve for X and Y. She would be sitting there, bouncing her knee and writing in purple pen, until, eventually, her heart would calm down. She'd trace the birthmark on her knee. She'd press her ear: the ringing was gone. So was the shimmer. She looked around and saw only a stack of paper plates for learning sine, cosine, tangent.

She had no trauma to match Natalie's, no questionable conduct to misconstrue. She thought about being a child: what had occupied her mind, whether her disposition might not have given her an edge, the radiance of madness or daring. What if the old her was gone, lost like the dungeons and captive dolls? Wrecked by normalcy and love, maybe she'd missed out when she could have endured a lot. How many chances did you get to know how special it was to hurt?

Dan Nief was not one of those chances, though Althea and Natalie agreed that going down on a girl was the epitome of baffling. What dizzy magic taught man that cursiving Dropkick Murphy's lyrics in a girl's vagina would get him sex? There was something bruinish about Dan. He wore a bumblebee flannel over his arm cuffs, loved the Singles soundtrack, and slurped. He wants me to know he's down there, Althea said. Um. I do. I know what I taste like, Natalie said after Althea told her about orgasming on WLTL. A sponge wiping up a cutting board of cantaloupe. Mmm, Althea said. Watery.

That became code when Natalie started dating Friel, when Althea moved onto Zerkel. Watery. Handsy. Chokey. Boyfriends came and went, dates over bread bowls, bowling alley coffee, basement math rock. They got almost serious, almost exclusive, almost I-Love-You before Althea and Natalie took over the relationship. What do you want? Althea wrote in the leopard notebook. To drink Friel like REGULAR Pepsi, Natalie wrote; :) haha to be so close to a person that even if just for a second you become them. I <3 you, Althea drew with the eraser head of her pencil; in No. 2 lead she bubble-lettered: LA.

La apartment, la city, la future, they wrote. They stanched their hunger for la later by laminating the present: It was more exciting recounting what they did than doing it. They spoke under their breath, engendered an aura, the particular haut monde of self-harm, and knew pain was more precious than a junior prom corsage. People say we're pretentious bitches who ruin boys' lives, Natalie reported in October, after Althea dumped Zerkel the morning of Homecoming. She was pretzel-legged on the carpet next to Althea in the study grotto of the library, surrounded by college brochures. It's going around the green room. Althea peeled a string off her celery and dropped it on her tongue. Boasting was boring, she thought. Brag with your body. Bones, cuts, good bruises—best were bruises. Blood maps. Hello, Natalie said, tapping Althea's knee. Does that matter to you? People are sensitive cunts, Althea said. Most boys deserve ruin. She sucked on her highlighter and tasted her own spit. Nothing will ever be like this, she wanted to say. Instead, she looked at her wish list of colleges. Being a snob means you know you're attention-worthy, Althea said. She patted Natalie's head. *Supercilium* is Latin for eyebrow.

Classmates may not have appreciated the vocabulary, but colleges did. Choices arrived. They'd both applied to schools in Los Angeles, but envelope by envelope their dream of living together dissolved. The definition of pathetic—i.e., queasily codependent—would've been applying to only the same places, but with decisions before them—nary a West Coast wait-listing; none, not even in kitty-corner states—it struck Althea that the universe might be against them. They'd been basted together, loosely, swiftly by circumstance; now it would be easy to rip them apart.

I'll email, Natalie said in August, the day before her parents drove her to Ohio. They were Diet-Pepsi-ing on the catwalk over 294, guarded on all sides by metal criss-crossing, puffing vanilla cloves and blowing sweet smoke into the exhaust-fleeced sky. Their cigarettes crinkled. I'll email every day. Her voice broke. Every goddamn day.

Let's be honest, Althea said. I probably won't.

Stop it, Natalie said. Not funny. She took out a pen and carefully wrote her new address on Althea's hand.

When she was done, Althea starfished her fingers and looked at it: Ohio zip code, .edu. Inside her skin, her bones became heavy. She stuck her fist in her pocket.

Not on purpose, she said. It'll just happen. Suddenly, she couldn't remember how to be a person. She heard herself. Phlegmatic. We'll trail off or I'll be dead—I'll be a beautiful dead princess without you.

I don't think that's funny.

What? You went to Florida and didn't send a postcard. Remember? I got slicey.

If you kill yourself, I kill myself, Natalie said. You can consider that a threat, okay? She dropped her cigarette into traffic. Do you have lip gloss?

Althea took out a tube. Natalie puckered her lips, the only fat part about her, and Althea painted her lips with thick gloppy strokes until they glistened and shone, glossy, wet, they were so, so pretty. Like the chicken pox scar on Natalie's chin. What were you supposed to do with this, everything you loved about someone? If you were only going to drift apart? Althea turned and looked out at the cars. Eight lanes, nine, with Ogden's on-offs. Constant, engulfing sound, like jamming your skull in a seashell or becoming the ocean.

Done, Althea said. She bit her tongue and put the tube back in her purse.

See? Perfect, Natalie said, rubbing her lips together. Don't be all death and gross. I'll email you, I'll call you. I'll send you a million letters. SWAK: Sealed. With. A. Kiss.

How often Althea had wondered if (no, when) this would happen. Here it was. She leaned forward until their sticky lips pressed, closer, touching, vanilla mouths melting on the grave candy of ash and Stargazer lilies pulverized in the gloss; she itsy-bitsy spidered up Natalie's neck and made a two-handed choker and squeezed her, pulled her closer. She was moaning, purring, quietly purring into Natalie's mouth, but it felt obligatory or onanistic or just weird. For the first time in years, Althea wished she were alone. Below, a fleshly truck driver shepherding a blue semi to Wisconsin laid on his horn.

#

Althea wrote first. A week into classes, she addressed a lavender envelope to Natalie the Beautiful, W-Box 1362. No reply. When two weeks had passed, she typed a rhapsodic email. There was St. Louis; the Forsyth dorm, brainy barista hunks, stone lions guarding the art museum; scrubby dreadlocked Karen, her RA who had a screed on the abuse of the word GIRL, as in, this is not an all girls' dorm; the GIRLS comparing stretch marks …i.e., NOT a pleasant stairwell activity; all that plus how lonely she was and was Natalie lonely, or hurting, or remembering all the bad things with Max all over again, too? Big changes trigger things, she wrote. PS. I hate life without you.

The email held its breath in her drafts folder until one midnight, dizzy after mandatory, suite-bonding Twister, she pressed SEND. Eleven days later, Natalie wrote back:

> Althea: Once a portraitist, always a portraitist. (Is that a word?) You should do my satire essay for the comp course I'm taking/being forced to take. It's called Precept, but that gilds the lily. Sorry about your dorm. I like my all-<u>GIRLS</u> floor. My roommate, Heather, and I started a tradition called Sunday Tea. We watch *Masterpiece Theatre* and drink—you guessed it—tea. With whiskey. Naughty sotties!
>
> ♥
>
> Natalie

Althea read it twice, nose so close to the computer screen that she smelled static electricity. It was time for lunch, but she skipped the cafeteria, bought a tube of peanuts and a can of Diet Pepsi from the Grab-n-Go cart, and went to the art building forty minutes early. She sat on a couch by the elevators, studying the top of her soda until it was time for class. Then she bent the pop tab back and forth, down the alphabet, and without forcing it, the tab came off at N. She left the peanuts behind a rubbery throw pillow.

How easily you vanished if you did not tribe with other girls. Without anyone to talk to, days began to pile up. They never happened. Fall semester, she went to class and took photographs in Forest Park, waiting for the raptor statues to come alive at sunset. She walked the unlit wooded trails and dared the world to send her menace from the bushes. Every time she got back to campus unscathed and climbed those three flights of stairs to her suite, she felt defeated to be alive. She ended the night with a movie. She watched at her wall-facing desk, in front of her hulking computer, blinds up, lights off, door locked. She must've replayed the tree scene in *Belle de Jour* fifty times, but *Requiem for a Dream* was on when her roommate came in, wearing a Cardinals visor and carrying a jack-o'-lantern, while onscreen one woman pegged another with a black dildo. For the rest of the semester, Althea had a single, and on Sunday afternoons, she wrote to Natalie. Natalie, enrobed in bergamot steam, tittering at *Masterpiece Theatre,* flicking crumpet crumbs off a cardigan. The emails began conversationally, deteriorated into sentiment, and plummeted toward accusations. I love you. I miss you. You're distant. You hate me. Tell me why. What did I do to you?

She sent a handful but by midterm gave up. She kept writing them, though, if only to reread them with the gluey, sordid fascination of an addict facing the mirror and recounting rock bottom.

Still, that December, Althea went home hopeful. Of course Natalie would call. She would invite her to the bowling alley for hot chocolate, half the cup whipped cream; she could hear her asking if she wanted to bundle up, take the Metra downtown, watch skaters wipe out on the rink at Navy Pier. None of that happened, and Althea was not surprised, and the more she explored how unsurprised she was, the more it stung. In the shower, she punched her hip bones until the flesh broke out in tiny red fireworks. She was so embarrassed—so stupid.

One afternoon, Althea and her mother went to buy a tree from the Boy Scouts' lot behind the high school. The sun was muddy pink, and the snow was hardly falling, dissolving before it hit your skin. How's Natalie? Evie asked, breaking a needle from a Douglas fir. Althea glanced at the machine that squeezed the trees in orange net. In London, she said, clearing her throat. Seeing *The Mousetrap*. That sounds nice, Evie said. She turned down the next aisle of trees, and Althea shut her eyes. She did not lie to her parents like this; she omitted things. She felt sick. The ringing in her ears was louder than Mariah Carey octaving on the radio, and over it or through it or despite it, her mother's voice: Would a blue spruce be too messy, Al? What do you think?

She did not think. She did not think or do much of anything for the entire rest of break. She wore purple fuzzy socks and shunned her parents until, on Christmas Day, the family ate guac, tacos, and mango flan before playing Taboo, a game Althea had been good at since third grade.

Still. It was not in her makeup to stay depressed. She realized this going back for spring semester, when she caught herself feeling clear, revived. She had hope. No matter how many harrowing movies she watched or poison epistles she penned, she had hope. In what? She didn't know; she didn't care.

She devoted herself to everything she could accomplish on her own. She bought binders. Threw out razors. Dyed her hair red. Took pictures of graffiti on the campus bridge. Stocked her mini-fridge with Diet Pepsi from Schnuck's. Brought a can-do attitude to isolation, a habit she saw no reason to break. Two years went by like this, an era she dubbed her stoic phase. She ate by herself and kept to herself and studied on her own and touched herself in a way she thought of as fucking herself and felt like a badass, superhero nun.

She was over her. She thought she was over her. March of junior year, she went through her in-box and deleted the few Natalie emails she had once received. They were gone with a click, and then everything was weird, like cutting your bangs. She stared at the screen, paused, and took a sip of Diet Pepsi. She X-ed out of her email. After thirty seconds, the word of the day screen-savered before her: PULE. There was a woolen clench in her throat, a deep burning hurt in her eyes; she was alone, and she didn't care if anyone reported her to the Dean of Student Life, if she scandalized the floor, let them hear her, she was a crier. She sobbed, for the first time in a long time. She saw Natalie, pictured her on the catwalk, a blurry wraith with famished eyes climbing a rope ladder tied to the trunk of an oak. Althea pushed her keyboard aside. She leaned forward, aimed her forehead, and threw herself at the desk. Her skull hit. She put her peace fingers between her eyebrows and felt for blood. None. She did it again. Again. And she felt like she'd bash a hole through the particleboard if she didn't see Natalie, so she took the Field's box off the high, deep shelf in her closet next to the tampons and brought it into her bed, where, sickened and touched by the one-track recklessness of her own heart, she pored over the photos. Most of them were from Edgemere—the stuffed cat's paws crossed in Natalie's lap, Natalie pouting; the cat perched on Natalie's head, Natalie rolling her eyes and smirking at Althea.

Her cranium throbbed. Eventually, cried out, she swept the photos into the box and closed it. The electricity was leaving her blood, and her blood was now just liquid in her brain. A benumbed comfort descended, and she remembered how she had adored blackouts and power outages as a child, dreamed of a life lit by kerosene lamps and rocky road ice cream you had to eat before it melted in the freezer. She blew her nose and put away the box.

It was senior year when she decided she was ready. She could experiment. All art students exhibited in the senior show. Althea had read about the Karen Carpenter movie Todd Haynes made with Barbies, and, after much hunting on the Internet and pestering of the media librarians who sat like eager puppies behind the peapod-shaped desk at Olin Library, she obtained a pristine VHS that she watched in one of the basement screening carrels, wearing a pair of headphones that smelled not unpleasantly like Orange Crush. Shortly after that, to the surprise of her parents, she took a five-hour train home. They were in the process of moving; Avery had retired, and they'd bought a two-bedroom condo that was a walk from the Music Box Theater and a short drive to the parish where Althea's brother was a priest. While her parents were picking up Thai, Althea went down to the basement. On the built-in benches that lined the walls, cardboard boxes printed with calla lilies, each neatly labeled in Evie's printing, held the aftereffects of the family. Patrick's toys. Althea's toys. Baby clothes 12–18 mos. She found the dinosaurs and her old dolls under a pod of stuffed seals and an ancient can of sweetened condensed milk.

There were the same noodles that night, and the easy prattle made her feel like an alien; Vouvray was the new sauvignon blanc. When's the screening? Evie asked. Middle of May, Althea said. Her mother licked a peanut off her lower lip. You know we're going to Le Puy then? What? Your brother's parish's pilgrimage. Avery refilled everyone's wine. He had started, she noticed, wearing a silver bracelet. The Sisters of St. Joseph were founded in Le Puy, France, he said. They saw women whose poverty was so threatening, they were desperate. They'd resorted to prostitution. The Sisters offered the women sanctuary. They shared the scripture and they taught them a skill. Tatting. In other words, making—. Lace, Althea said, brusquer than she meant. I know what tatting means. We'll be there through the middle of June, Evie said. It's good that you're here. We wanted to …well, we didn't want to ask over the phone. Althea speared her chopstick through a scallion and dragged it around on her plate. Would you be disappointed if we weren't at graduation? Althea looked around the room. Her mother's latest painting hung on the wall across from the short end of the table. It was a departure, Evie had said earlier: a thatched-roof cottage before a misty pond where four swans glided. Of course not, Althea said. I don't even really want to walk. She sipped her wine. In that bucolic cottage, there were rapist farmers, she decided. Pitchforks, hoes, shovels …the poor swans. She listened to her mother explain serendipity (France! Coinciding with their thirtieth wedding anniversary!) and waited to feel angry. Anger is good, her Lighting II professor said, anger you can use. If she had wanted her parents to ask about her idea for the film, if she had wanted them to know what she was obsessed with, she would've been angry. She didn't, so she wasn't. Her parents were thoughtful people.

The next morning, she left, her backpack too lumpy to wear. She sat in the business class car of a train to St. Louis eating cold spring rolls and storyboarded the entire ride. She glanced out the window at the shadowy, scarecrow towns in southern Illinois. She caught herself stuck there, grinning at her own reflection in the window, her mouth rictal and awkward, criminal, like someone hatching a heist. She felt giddy off the fumes of staged retribution.

The film came together quickly. She had taken a few classes. She knew basic animation and editing. To obtain footage, she did not need much more than a room with a door and a table, conditions she found easily: she did all of her shooting in an old halfway house that the Art Department had nicknamed the Hatch and repurposed into a student workspace. Her name was chalked on the door of an area with walls the color of strawberry milk and a concrete floor. The door had a padlock. She left the dinosaurs, the dolls, equipment, small props, and the Field's box inside her studio.

The whole building was key-coded, but she didn't like being away from her project. She did not like returning to her dorm, work unfinished. She couldn't rest. She couldn't sleep. In bed, she found herself thinking about Edgemere, and Natalie, and the baked gloom of summer, pudding in the cafeteria, plaiting blades of grass. Then she would wake up; in the mornings, she'd arrived as though by red-eye. Dreamless, direct. If she got to the Hatch late, she'd catch other people talking in the kitchen, where the Mr. Coffee was always juiced. The sociable art students needed to go on, sound smart to raise themselves onto that shaky platform of confidence and focus: That's mischaracterizing her. She's not dark at all. Everything's dark. Not especially. Read Mulvey: you can't escape girls on film being girls caught on film. Scopo—wrong. Althea slipped into her studio and shut the door. There was a stuffed tabby on her worktable, and she put the animal on her head. She faced the tripod and closed her eyes.

His name was Max, she said in her best Natalie voice. *Truth or Dare?*

A week before the screening, Althea went to the mail room and found a slip in her mailbox; at the window, she traded it for a package, a padded envelope larger than a newspaper. There was no sender listed, and her own name was typed out in a coltish, serif font. She opened it in her room, took out the contents, and leaned it against her headboard. She sat at the foot of the bed and looked at it. From another room on the floor, she heard the opening of "Eight Days A Week." It was a color photograph inside a sharp-cornered black frame. A lawn rolled out, sumptuous as a bolt of green velvet. In the foreground, a robin perched on the bowl of a concrete birdbath, its crescent breast glittering with water. Beyond that, Althea recognized a Skip-It, tossed in the grass like an oversized bubble wand. In the background, there was an enormous tree with a vast branch span and a castle sprouting out of the leafy cleft in its trunk, red and yellow pennants garlanding the ramparts. Two children stood in front of the trunk, holding their hands up in a victory V. The boy was a buzz-cut smudge. The girl could best be represented by a sparsely whiskered calico cat. The note on the back was typed in the same font as the envelope label, on a piece of paper smaller than the package slip. Parents sent this from neighbors. Me and the Monster. Thought you'd want to see him after all these years. The Beatles became Pearl Jam. Althea slid off her bed and opened her email. It was the only thing to do.

For the screenings, Althea dressed up in a vegan leather skirt that hit just above the knee and an utterly Natalie turtleneck. She hurried across campus. Her Chelsea boots clacked through the portico and down the wide stairs, and she thought how she sounded like a person of distinction coming, even if she was hugging her elbows. It was a warm, purple night, with a perfect half-moon tacked to the sky. A word for twilight, she thought, head ducked. Crepuscule. A voice in her head said, Use it or lose it, babe. She pressed the emerald in her ear and walked toward the contemporary art museum, an angular, glassy building that looked like a skyscraper deconstructed and reassembled by chance.

She went inside. With its vaulted ceilings and stark walls, the foyer usually gave off a discomfiting austerity, but now the space glowed with champagne. The graduating artists, their housemates and classmates and parents and siblings and professors and boyfriends and girlfriends from other states and countries thronged around tables of cheese and fruit and crackers and, off to the left, a cake stand of Peeps. Althea scanned the crowd, caught the eye of no one she knew, and held her mouth firmly shut. She got a glass of red wine and went into Theater B. Her director's chair was marked, the second seat from the left end of the front row. There would be a Q&A to follow each film. She picked up the program and read her name, Althea Zafaris, *These Things Happen*.

With the program to her chest, she stood there, looking back at the fifty chairs that soon would fill. A windbreaker here, a hobo bag there, the sort of weathered suede satchel she'd never been able to pull off, and soon, if she trusted the email, the ticket number, the train schedule, the arrival time, that element of grace that glanced on the world, Natalie. What would she look like, how would she smell, where would they begin, and why would they end this time? A strange laugh tickled Althea. She saw a shimmer—she was staring into the projector. She turned around and imagined her dolls, their hair moussed, their nippleless volcano breasts and placid crotches encompassing the screen. And then, what they'd force on the men. The men, the dinosaurs: the power of zoom in was that, close enough, a hole was a hole, and anything going in too rough was torture. In her head, Althea rehearsed the answer to the only question she was sure someone would ask her: How can this be true? She could almost hear the wheedling voice of ignorance, fat on Ritz and amity. When I was a girl, I practically lived at my neighbors', she would begin. There was a boy. Max. She cracked her knuckles and sat down, crossing one leg over the other, so the knee with the birthmark was on top.

Something Real

My dream date? We've been flirting for weeks in diffused, functional situations. Classrooms, offices, the steps leading down to his basement. I admire his jeans: the slash in the knee or the way the back pockets lie flat on his ass. He's still young enough for a receding hairline to look hot. And then there's the dumb shit you're already expecting: I want his square jaw to stamp me down. I imagine him saving me and then revealing unreal truths about himself—arrests in the lacerating sunrise. A series of skillfully hosted parties where men and women alike spew, spill, split inside and outside of moving vehicles, with or without leather interiors, with or without disarming rap, with or without recognizable samples. His eyes change colors according to my mood ring. Darlings, these are my badges. I'm a skilled scout risking it all in fake eyelashes. There's been a campfire and a successful journey into the jungle. We've trapped hares, jerboas. Or, maybe. Maybe, we're in a galaxy where gravity does great things for my tits. And with him looking at me, I feel just right.

If I were a sob story that could make an intake counselor cry. If I were a meal designed for a compartmentalized plate. If I were a cognitive reframing technique. If I were a cue. If I were a creative outlet for cruddy cravings. If I were a rhyme scheme. A young lady who made the acquaintance of a fine gen. With a facility for dissociative logic. Perched on the flagpole during the pledge in study hall. If I were a length of time, I'd be how long? Which season? Whose theoretical achievement? A meme or a phoneme?

Late in the game, we're leasing a condo with frosted blue windows. A marble countertop made of recycled materials like broken bottles translates into patches of glass like shooting stars. The balcony with the breeze and the beach. His walk-in closet and my rack of marabou mules. It's like I've been waiting on this my whole life. Take off your face, he says in his dreamiest voice, aren't you hungry yet? Guided visualization has been proven to have a positive effect on reducing behaviors: He's wearing a button-down and a blazer but no tie, he's sitting on the edge of the bed, he's growing out his hair in a way that makes us both squirmy. I'm in a slip and skinny heels, entranced by my reflection—parts of my body push against the silk, and my hands are moving up and down my thighs, rubbing my ribs. Eyes closed, mouth agape. Enough already, he says, and yanks me into the bathroom. Beside the sink, a trash can filled with stained cotton balls. All the removers reek like variations on the French 75. So long, liquid liner! I pucker up and print pouts on the Kleenex. I bat and preen and pose. Don't be a tease, he says, standing behind me, cuffing my neck, breathing on the tattoo that traipses from the bottom of my bob to the tip of my tailbone, look at me.

Mansion, apartment, shack, house. Rumor has it she stores her tampons in the freezer or a lockbox. Her first time was in an elevator—on a football field—on the high dive—coming down from the flu while her parents were out of town—her nose ground into the carpet on a staircase (musty, dandered), her wrists bound behind her back with one of those bandanas he always wore to keep his curls under wraps.

We've got this bad habit of losing ourselves in the bedroom for hours at a time, stippling sunny scenes of parasol people parading across our stomachs with smelly markers. We're into things seeping into our skin. When we roll around, we smear the sheets magenta and turquoise. This is an afternoon of candy and cake. In other words, afterwards, we get stoned and watch snakes have at it on the big screen mounted on the wall like easy art. Are you eating? he asks me. I've got a few tubes of Smarties sorted by color on a white saucer on the bedside table. He's drinking Grey Goose and Gatorade through a Twizzler. It doesn't look right, I say when the diamondback unhinges its jaw. Lifting my ponytail up like a thought bubble (Aha! Oooh baby! Oh yeah!), he asks me, How do you feel?

If he were a way for the world to end. If he were a perfume. If he were an article of clothing. If he were an ethnic cuisine. If he were a way to get kicked out of the house. If he were a summer vacation. If he were a telephone solicitor. If he were a sex act. If he were a form of childhood humiliation.

At a house party in the more affluent suburb adjacent to our own, I am surrounded by too many slumber party sluts. So I wear a white wifebeater and a miniskirt with an eyelet hem. So I smoke a bowl before showing up and I'm a lowlife, my mother tells me all the time. I'm a lowlife with a love life (lie) and a lowly B-F (so not true) that I loof-love-loaf ever so—so. Not. So here's the filmed future: We're drinking Bud Light bought by someone's brother and chewing massive potato chips explosive with grease, we're dancing to clanking hip-hop, it's my cunt and the host's cock, we're not pretending I don't feel him pressing into me when I'm dancing with my ass pressed into him, we're not pretending that I don't feel his cock crawling up the crease, we're not pretending that the pressure doesn't reassure us, we're not pretending that his mother doesn't have a vibrator in her top dresser drawer, we're not pretending that I don't tend to end up in compromising situations. So I'm at the house party, I'm catching up with the cameras, and a little later I see myself—supine Sleeping Beauty and wherefore art thou whilst disrobement—whilst cigarettes and spread crevices—whilst Sharpied hearts and stars scrawled across the scar from the one summer the doctors could've sworn it was some disease that begins with a G, but negative twenty pounds later (oh, a girl longs for the liquid diet, longs for liquid, try it, long enough on all liquids and she's a diet longing herself) they split her open and cranked out the diagnosis, wham-o, bam-o, done deal, ma'am, mama, lady with the new lease on life, little girl with the extra special curl. So it was me on a bed and a cigarette stuck in my vagina and words scribbled across my stomach and three to five guys until my body was weak from coming in my sleep. So relax. Take a chill pill. The female body has been known to writhe in weirder whereabouts. You don't cry when you're passed out. You're not an erasure of pleasure. You feel good, you feel great, you feel wonderful, you feel yes, you feel more, you feel yes, nice and slow, you feel oozing and blue screening, you feel everything, you feel zero zip nada nothing when you're not looking.

I dreamt he asked me what I wanted for my eighteenth birthday. I said I wanted to see the Virgin Mary. Have you been eating? he asked. Had I? I'd been three meals plus snacks ever since I left the hospital. Boring, boring, boring. By the time nine o'clock rolled around, I couldn't pinch myself into wakefulness before the football game or the sitcom or the teenage drama where the ocean throbbed into every scene like a blue vein. Yeah, I've been eating, I said. He fed me. His favorite possession was a transatlantic cookbook. To simplify: Whose preparation produces a better steak au poivre? The perfect green salad. We ate radicchio and Boston Bibb tossed in lemon and olive oil, erupting with radishes and haricots verts and extra frisée; then spinach salad doused in warm bacon dressing studded with pomegranate arils. He was making his way through the whole book just for me. With the table between us, I was dissecting the consumables he collected. How does it taste? he asked. We sat in front of a window that revealed Lake Michigan was a long-term lover, a leech, a sleaze. A body of taffeta capped with white carnations. Nothing feels right when you're looking at me, I said. I *wasn't* eighteen anymore, I reminded him.

Long jogs along the lakefront led her to cataclysmic con-
clusions about certain channels in her life. She could finally
make out the lyrics to her favorite songs. She stopped mistaking mixed signals. She didn't need to eat anything edible.
She swallowed dimes and had great sex and texted all her exes
when he left town for a wedding in Las Vegas. She did an extra
mile gaping at the Drake and imagined her neck creaking with
Chanel costume jewelry from the boutique—pearl necklaces
stopped with enamel charms and clip-on camellias. Running
along the lake was disarmingly similar in winter or summer.
Stillness with snow. Stuck in the sand. There were yachts and
booze cruises and Ferris wheels and boathouses, long docks
she always ran to the edge of, in another state, another town,
on vacation when she was much younger, there was a museum
caught in a lighthouse, a restaurant responsible for her first and
only case of food poisoning (she'd been five, there was smoked
salmon spread, she puked a sinkful of pink in the black-and-
white bathroom of the bed-and-breakfast where sachets of
Queen Sophia kept her sniffling for a week). So she got liq-
uid-oriented when he left.

He takes me on a casino date after we stop for cash, but we end up crawling around the back seat. This is years after we're caught in the parking lot by the man throttling his cock. Even once the cops came, we couldn't help ourselves. We tried to stop the best we could, but our bodies were potions. There was no turning back. Now we're into late arrivals, laid out from too much acid. He wears straight pants and a rakish shave. This is during my fat phase where all my clothes end up on the ground. It doesn't feel right without you looking at me, he said, when I insisted on keeping my eyes shut. Or I'd been wrapped in a blanket in the bathroom for hours before we decide to lose our loot. My eyes were covered by a velour tie. I was seeing navy. I kept my eyes open. I felt the fibers.

She shops way too much, but maybe it's alright for her to drive to the health club in the middle of the night. You're asleep on the couch before she's out of the garage after another meal where she's not hungry and you're chasing Christmas cookies with a neat single malt before anyone's served. She wants the hot tub to cook her kinky constructs. You want a luminous skull to pose just so. She's the type of girl who leaves her bags in the back seat, tags flag each garment in your closet, like, *Are we running a coat check around here?* This should be the part about total bliss and the Forelle pear you're letting rot in your studio, but the streets are stuffed with snow: maybe it's worthwhile to let her get cashed in a bikini. Maybe you think about her too much. Maybe she hands her ID to the attendant and he swipes her in. Maybe three old men glued to the couch in the foyer flash gold watches. This is an omen. There are high ceilings and marble floors. She fingers her earrings. You feel adult. She feels aware. You feel accountable. Then she's in the locker room, in a changing stall, naked and tying. She brings a flask. She doesn't shower first. She doesn't wear a towel. She walks to the hot tub barefoot. She slips in dry. She puts her ponytail on the ledge, she sees the Virgin, the heat is a veil, she administers the dosage, you control the jets. She expects the current will just about leave her bankrupt.

Who weighs what? The vertical? The TKO? The rebounds? The fouls? Feeding my slips into the slot at the redemption station, I'm Bacardi Limon and zoning. There's a giant television. Buck breakfast where I break down and order bacon. Or, alternately, an assemblage of Somebodies screw me in the cab of a Chevy pickup until the steering feels right. I've realized it before: nothing after years of spectatorship except for, every once in a while, when the moon is a shiner against the sky, dozens of men in baseball hats populate my fantasies, all of them lean and ropy, nothing too extreme, consonant muscles, extracurricular ballplayers, the sort of guys who'd meet up for a game in Brookfield and, afterwards, unwind over Murphy's Law cocktails at Irish Times.

I crossed my legs and pictured us slumming in a studio space where we lived next door to a mystic named Steve who ran an online university from his one bedroom. A dingy town and a former business college. Were we absorbing the ghosts of pupils past? Nights, the streets swarmed with laid-off Maytag men and railroad conductors and girls strengthened by steak suppers. We'd wake up to find mailboxes uprooted. Trash cans overturned. We were so poor, I was biting my tongue all week and tapping his arm to the tempo of my iPod. Each of us with an earbud jammed canalwards. Mornings we stayed in bed without touching, stilling our inhalations, staring at the ceiling or a new set of breezy flowered curtains billowed by sunlight. If our blood took a breather and our stomachs didn't grumble and I stopped hearing my eyelashes sashay every time I blinked, Steve would unfurl sounds like ragged garland. I rolled onto my stomach and bit the pillow. Do you feel all right? he asked.

She wanted to be held down. She wanted an abrupt confrontation. She wanted the bathroom attendant to give her a strawberry Blow Pop or some gum that would kill her cravings for real meals. She wanted someone to grip her face in the middle of a kiss. There would be angels sputtering and a dead streetlight, and the car's heat would knock them around, and the slot in her wallet where she kept her license would be empty—she'd be in barrettes and drop-waisted dresses screened with costumed teddy bears. Without flinching, she'd devote days to drawing girls and mermaids. Sewing lumpy pillows. Then, she realized how the time you spent thinking never returned. The words between lovers dissolved like sloughed skin. She felt good about nihilism and novas. Just thinking of her consciousness zooming unfettered through space (her license dangling from the immaterial like a gift tag) sent her into a trance. She began frequenting graveyards with men twice her age. The courtships blossomed on the subway, and the outings were orchestrated through the post. The men wore black leather jackets and pressed gray jeans. Their bodies looked like dried fruit stored in the refrigerator too long. But she moved in, cozied up, got close. Bright blue bruises starred her body's most valuable parts. Against white sheets, she saw black hairs; in the shower, she tasted their skin like sour melon; and, at odd times, like while pouring cereal, she smelled bones levigating. She didn't know if it was her or them.

After my last high school dance I was already missing the days when I would peer into my parents' toilet after I'd spilt my guts and cleaned up the mess like there was something to augur in the oily residue shimmering across the surface. I'd have prayer candles burning on both sides of the sink, the box of long matches out (I'd pilfered them during my last year altar serving), getting heady while the smoke streamed up, leaving a pale black tongue on the mirror, the pink tiles, and the framed photo collage of flamingos. Maybe it was that one Christmas where I went gaga over the gag that made me feel like a gathering of angels. All the blood vessels in my eyes burst. The whites disappeared. In a dark office, with a lead cape over my chest, a doctor said I could've gone blind. If pain is a blood blister smaller than a baby's nostril.

Alone she ran seven miles instead of six. She ate rolls of black pepper turkey covered in pink sea salt while she cooked. Running a knife along the rib, she deleafed rainbow chard. She pretended color mattered. She diced the remaining ribs and cooked those longer. She peeled four parsnips. Chopped smaller than coins, the parsnips boiled as she showered. She didn't condition. An old razor. Simmered with water and olive oil, the chard left behind a pink broth. She stirred in currants. She pureed the parsnips with vanilla and butter, white pepper and cream. So, look: She only lied about one ingredient. Diagramming the plate teaches the patient to portion. To quantify balance. Visualize appetite.

I dreamt we went to a gallery opening. It was my ex-boyfriend's show. I'd dated an artist. I'd dated an artist who shot big sheets of metal and peeled back the rough edges so ruffles formed where the bullet went through. All his pieces had parts that got really pretty where there'd been penetration. The bullet maybe the most banal. There was his arm shoved through a pane of glass, or my pinky finger working a wider hole in a sheet of hot sugar. Look at me, I said. This is the girl I used to be. I used to be this girl. He held a plastic cup of wine and a water cracker smeared with Brie, and he watched the television set inside a glass box and saw the tip of my black-and-white finger blistering before our eyes thanks to the wonder of living at high speed or maybe the trust fund the artist had accessed after years of pleading with his parents. You look like yourself but different, he said. I think that's dream logic, I said. Are you hungry? He assembled a plate with a smattering of snacks. All I ate was an olive.

It was winter break, and my friends were vacationing on islands fragrant with summer air. It was me and a boy with his parents, watching a movie where two girls solve a gruesome crime. Silhouettes jitterbugged, and up-close commissures lurched into pleasure. We were sitting on different cushions of the same ratty couch. I was cross-legged, then legs crossed at the knee. He stood up once, in class, to toss a wad of gum in the trash, and I watched him walk. Then I started running as my own private extracurricular. I'd always been attracted to narratives of self-improvement and epiphany. My best friend drove me home from the train station, and I'd change out of my uniform into gym shorts from junior high and a sports bra and a snug hooded sweatshirt and, gripping my Discman like a frisbee, I'd do three to five miles just so the next day I'd be able to get through the period where he drummed like a fiend, tapped his checkered Vans to a silent rhythm, ate unflattering snacks, brushed his long bangs out of his face, emanated patchouli, complimented a poem for being *homogenous*. Turns out, all the hottest high school boys like to drum on their desks. Wear layers. Write elegies to George Harrison. Maybe it hit me when he died. Our teacher played the acoustic of "While My Guitar Gently Weeps" and we sat in silence, lights off, and I couldn't go anywhere.

She just wanted him to get hard. He just wanted a few extra feet. She just wanted easy blow jobs at halftime or an
orgasm-less go in the Jacuzzi with him looking at her. He
wanted to record her in the throes of an unwanted encoun-
ter. Have you eaten? he asked. There was never a question of
whether he could do it without making serious eye contact
with the camcorder. He plugged her in and went to work.

Talk dirty. Pretend you're a dyke. Pretend you're a fat chick. Pretend you're a corpse. You wear your hair short. I put my ponytail in my mouth. Are you—*hungry?* It's like I'm sucking on my grandfather's badger shaving brush. I puff out my stomach and picture pounds of starchy choices—potatoes pasted with cheese, corn pudding, and pasta. Or maybe I'm teeming with triplets. Or I tongue my gums and try to touch each taste bud as though it's the pebbly inside of my girl's pussy—we're two buxom babes in the back of a van, this vanity of vanities, all-is-vanity shit. He makes a mirror out of not-so-thin air. Or I shave my head.

When it's a minor game, there's no posture more permissible than his head tipped back. His throat collecting stubble. The sportscasters incanting reenactments like psalms. Without any eye contact, he doesn't say anything about looking right or feeling without. He's wearing jeans and a white undershirt. Are you hungry? he asks. Not much. She wanted him to hold her ponytail while she took up all of halftime taking him to the edge. She wanted a frigid glance. Grit and clench. Alley, ankles quavering, wristbones banged against brick. Bruising her bad enough for tomorrow to be teeming with party favors, souvenirs, mementos, keepsakes, for Pete's sake, scar a girl, why don't you—race her to think brink, don't think twice.

So there was the response on the note, circle one, circle both, yes or no. Her stomach growled as though a small rodent were scratching and fighting in there, as though she were in for a blackout bash, as if everything could be traced back to that particular incident at the club with the bathroom attendant and the drugged drink and that bandage dress she loved that made her legs look longer than they already were—he told her they made him hungry. So, she never let a guy eat her out on the first or second date. So, she didn't really believe sexologists who linked female narcissism and needing it so bad, your teeth started to chatter. She'd never attended a circus with erotic acrobatics. The only big breasts she'd seen were in terrible pornos. Suds and lusty Hausfraus. Something mulled, something with wine. She epiphanied like a female figure from a film looking for some sort of self-discovery at a foreign floral convention or a monastery—all set to an airy soundtrack dropping notes like stones into a blank pond without any husband to be had, just strangers and sushi on long white plates. Yes or no. They slow danced, and he told her to go suck an egg.

Once she attended a motorcycle show with her father. At Mc-Cormick Place they were oohing and aahing. Her father wasn't in the market for a new bike. She digested bold paint and custom decals, the intestinal metal of engines and fenders. Foot pegs and handlebars, leather workers in fringed chaps, and girls with buoyantly hard breasts in fluorescent bikinis—highlighter hues—could easily consume a day. Do you want to eat? her father asked her. They walked around with hotdogs in paper boats to catch the relish and mustard that squirted out with each bite. There was red and yellow and dirty green. They drank Coke and chewed crushed ice. There was brown and black and clear and white. Turbine, carburetor, piston. She couldn't remember the right name for any part.

With an older boyfriend, I'll go to the cemetery. We'll look at his ancestors. I'll cross my arms over my chest, and the oysters beneath my eyes will deflate. It's autumn and I wear a black coat with an asymmetrical zipper, the bias—well, I don't think about what I wear any more than I think about what *he* wears (pointy-toed loafers and blacks jeans): Something about it just *works*. It isn't like my last boyfriend. We are not that couple. The air in the cemetery blows gray film over everything—statues of the Virgin, crosses, dyed pink baby's breath sprays. He stops at a cluster with his last name. He's twice my age, Dutch, and from a family that came to America before it was America. I feel conscious of my heritage as though I'm filling out a census or a standardized test with a set of sex-specific convictions, but when he kneels in front of a plain marker, I lower my eyes and speed through the rosary in my pocket. This is my mother, he says at the last stone and opens his backpack. It's filled with Fiji Water and satsuma mandarins. I unzip my purse and take out long matches, the prayer candles someone has left under the sink in my apartment. He sets the fruit out on the stone and empties several liters of water. For years now, I've been stalking the graveyards in my family's Michigan. I've been a proponent of novenas. I set a candle near the stone and strike a match. He kisses me and pulls my hair. This is all there is for you to see, he says, looking right at me. A square of lace covers my hair.

She liked Sunday afternoons spiraling into substance abuse. They would watch football and start drinking beer. With the artist, a vegan who still sucked her off even when she said no, she'd go through premium tequila and Grand Marnier and bags of limes. Now, all she wanted was to pop the cap off a bottle. She didn't want a glass. She'd take a can. She liked the way his face got loose from booze. He liked losing track of time. He asked her to check the clock and tell him when a half hour had passed. Sometimes they talked about their favorite commercials, but mostly she sat with patience dissolving on her tongue like the Eucharist. She had a lot to make up for. Bouts of Ordinary Time when she'd pasted the moistened Body of Christ to the underbelly of the pew. Because who knew the calories. During confessions, she'd even created a hypothetical friend who couldn't stop herself from doing the same thing, and the pastor told her that the Lord understood sickness. Compulsion. Pass along a penance—twenty Hail Marys. She was older than she wanted to acknowledge, but younger than anything really terminal, and when she couldn't keep track of her heart rate, she raced through her prayers—or, fine, sometimes she prayed while she gave head. While he fucked her and she chewed at the sheets like a bit. Or she imagined a gag.

I'm a comet, I'm an asteroid, I'm a nova. He's walking by every night. He's driving around the block. He's standing in front of the bed. He's pointing at a couple pots on the front burners. He's showering. He's using too much conditioner. He's bringing a health kit heavy on the moisturizers. I don't feel right, he says without looking at me. I'm kind of hectic inside. But we decide to ride the elevators to the top floor of my building and shimmy up a service ladder that leads to the roof, pockets sagging with bottles and snacks, so I'm Sabrina but without the tennis court or Veuve Clicquot, the groundskeeper father or the French education, the black-and-white ball gown or the flutes molded after Marie Antoinette's décolletage—still, he helps me up from the top rung, and we look out over the city as fireworks coruscate like somewhere someone's battering birthstones. We sit on his spare sweatshirt. We drink lambic. We look at birds nesting in strange spaces.

We met-cute. Everything seemed right when he was looking at me. When I looked at him, we both said alright. Alright. He intimated himself to me. I played coy. It seemed promising: I wasn't wearing my hair like a flapper or styling myself after a macrobiotic sitcom sweetheart. I was never hungry, and he never asked, but there were shifts in power and costume changes and setting negotiations—the first grip had family in Baltimore, but the writer'd always imagined a Midwestern romcom, and then there was the prima donna lead who just wanted to do it in San Francisco to be near her gay best friend who still lived in the Castro, an old queen without anything amorous to show for all his adventures in life—and the soundtrack was really cohesive—it blew us all away—somehow, we heard grandiose and classic, hip and heartbreaking in every song. Really, even the score was genius. After takes, there were beers against a backdrop of haggard men and women and bathrooms the size of closets where nobody considered anybody's body in a shallow, unhallowed manner and quiet walks in hazy light where I brushed his hand or he bumped my hip, and our hair commingled, and we were making eye contact that said, here, right now, this is going somewhere. The copy was good, and no one stole the show. It was sweet and smart and sexy and true.

I knew nothing was going to happen.

Acknowledgments

The earliest of these stories tore out of long Galesburg nights, train whistles ringing through the fog. I am forever thankful to: Barbara Tannert-Smith, for believing in the static mass in the distance. To Monica Berlin, for tenderness and faith and deep-blue marginalia.

To Robin Metz, for summoning a lioness and telephoning the hospital: I miss you.

To Hache, for teaching me to read and teaching me to teach; for saying 'formalist,' 'stylist,' 'a symbol is a stone,' 'cariño,' for your black tickets of faith and support: I miss you.

For inspiration, instruction, and incredible patience: Kellie Wells, Kathryn Davis, Marshall Klimasewiski, Amanda Goldblatt, Chris Dennis, Alison Espach, Sara Flannery Murphy, and Mike Bezemek. Thank you for accepting the sentences and the sugar. Alec Hershman: for your linguistic hijinks and your faith in the messy mischief of work. To Eileen G'Sell: I raise a Mata Hari. To Kathleen Finneran, for demonstrating stillness and poise amidst the tumult.

To brilliance in The Valley, Hannah Brooks-Motl, Dan Bevacqua, Noy Holland, Sam Michel, Dara Wier, and Peter Gizzi.

To the writers who make my email worth checking. Donald Rogers and everyone in The Writing Room: Andrew Mac-Donald, Erin Pienaar, Melissa Carroll, and more.

"The cinema is not a slice of life, but a piece of cake," said Alfred Hitchcock. Thank you to Wendy McCredie and Leonard Schulze, for a great many cakes—plus. To Marcos McPeek Villatoro, for your rigor and warmth. To my students and colleagues at Mount Saint Mary's University, for the charism and community.

Shannon Buckley and Courtney Napleton: thank you for teaching me the art of obsession.

Love and appreciation, always, to Mom and Dad, Gary and Jacqueline.

To Nova, for your big, big sweetness.

My deepest gratitude, eternally, to Thomas Cook, partner in a life free of loafing. "Do you want to read a story?"

\#

I am grateful to the editors of the publications where many of these stories first appeared:
"The Wait," *The Paris Review*
"Meaningful Work," *BOMB*
"Cake Eater," *FENCE*
"The Scar," *The New Orleans Review*
"Service," *Caketrain*
"Lamb, Goat, Tongue," *Bennington Review*
"Ratchet," *Black Warrior Review*

"Litter," *Subtropics*
"Clambering Over Such Rocks," *Gulf Coast*
"Lisa Is the Water," *Joyland*
"The Quiz and the Pledge," *Passages North*
"Acacia," *The Arkansas International*
"Rio Grande, Wisconsin," *Day One*
"Anniversary," *PANK*
"These Things Happen," *Alaska Quarterly Review*
In a slightly altered form, *Something Real* was published as a chapbook by Dancing Girl Press.